CONVOY

The biggest book, the biggest movie, the biggest story ever told about a breed of men who decide to screw the system and stand up for their rights – even if it means a whole load of trouble afterwards.

LET ’EM ROLL

B. W. L. Norton

Convoy

CORGI BOOKS
A DIVISION OF TRANSWORLD PUBLISHERS LTD

CONVOY

A CORGI BOOK 0 552 10647 X

First publication in Great Britain

PRINTING HISTORY
Corgi edition published 1978

This book is set in Intertype Baskerville

Corgi Books are published by
Transworld Publishers Ltd,
Century House, 61–63 Uxbridge Road,
Ealing, London W5 5SA

Made and printed in Great Britain by
Cox & Wyman Ltd,
London, Reading and Fakenham

CONVOY

PROLOGUE

The giant tank lumbered into position on the northern approach to the bridge. It was an M-60A2, one of the most advanced prototypes, not usually assigned to the National Guard, but this was a crack unit, the best in Texas and sure to be the first called up in any national emergency.

While the men on the tank completed their final course and range adjustments, the rest of the squad fanned out into the rocks and scrub on either side of the road.

"Damned if I know what we're doing here," one of them wondered aloud, "This ain't no war."

"Shut your face, man," his buddy ordered curtly. "Listen."

From the distance came the low-pitched rumble of powerful engines approaching rapidly like a summer storm. The noise sent a wave of activity through the two Texas State Police cars and single-armored riot control vehicle that were backing up the action across the bridge.

Suddenly a black Mack diesel came roaring around the curve and semi-jackknifed to a stop about fifty yards from the tank guarding the bridge. Before the dust had a chance to completely settle, another M-60A2 pulled around the bend behind the truck, effectively cutting off any escape to the rear. Behind this second tank was a line of big rig diesels that stretched back around the curve and out of sight. In the abrupt silence that followed, the giant machines seemed to be holding each other at bay like prehistoric animals.

"It's him alright," the Guardsman spoke again. "Look at the hood on that truck."

The hood ornament on the Mack had been replaced by a rubber Woolworth-type duck, identifying the driver as their quarry, the man whose spirit and determination had brought them all – the police, the truckers, the National Guard, even the FBI – to this time and place – The Rubber Duck.

The Police P.A. suddenly sounded from across the river: "Surrender. Surrender immediately or you will be fired on."

Inside the cab, the Duck turned to Melissa. Now more than ever, her thoroughbred good looks seemed woefully out of place. She should be photographing this action, not part of it.

"You better get out," he said softly.

"What are you going to do?"

As she waited for his answer, Melissa noticed how tired the Duck had become, not just from the events of the last couple of days, but from the years and miles on the road, too many miles, strange women, strong drink that had creased his face like a map. His amphetamine-triggered eyes darted over the situation like a snake's tongue, but he only said, "Better go."

"You will be fired upon unless you surrender," the P.A. broke in. "You have ten seconds. One . . . two . . ."

The Duck cracked the door on Melissa's side of the cab and pushed her gently toward it.

"But what are you going to do, Duck?" she demanded as part of the answer began to hit her.

He took in the scene one more time – the tanks, the police, the squad of men lining the road. Then his eyes came back to hers, asking her to understand.

"Keep on truckin. Now git."

"Seven . . . eight . . ."

Slowly, feeling very old and useless, Melissa climbed out of the cab and walked away. She heard the door slam behind her but didn't look back. She didn't want to see what was coming.

"Ten," the P.A. rasped. "This is your final chance. Come out with your hands over your head."

The tense silence was broken by a sudden Indian war-whoop which in turn was drowned out by the roar of four hundred diesel horses as the Duck put the hammer down. The black Mack shot forward, charging certain death, the tank directly ahead.

Inside the tank Corporal Elton Beauregard racked his .50 caliber M-1 HMG and prepared to fire. The crazy son of a bitch was going to get blown away, right now. The radio crackled, "This is Colonel Ridgeway. Hold your fire. This is a police action. I repeat, do not fire unless ordered to do so."

As the truck approached the bridge, Duck threw himself to the floor of the cab, steering blindly with his left hand. If he had calculated correctly there might be just enough room.

Almost miraculously, the truck wedged cleanly between the tank and the retaining wall of the bridge, striking both at once and tearing off its fender and doors. But somehow it was through and heading across the bridge toward the scattering police forces on the far side.

Almost immediately, the M-60 machine gun mounted on the riot car opened up. In a matter of seconds the Mack's windshield disappeared and steam began pouring from its punctured radiator. But it kept coming with no sign of slowing despite the terrible punishment. It was moving through.

Inside the cab a bullet had ripped through Duck's arm. But intent on steering and punching the gas pedal, he felt no pain or fear. A pure, perfect rage was his shield against all that.

Suddenly an officer wearing an Arizona Sheriff's uniform leaped to the top of the car and took control of the gun. He centered it on the VOLATILE CHEMICALS sign stencilled across the leading edge of the trailer. He muttered something that sounded like, "Blow, you asshole," and pressed the firing mechanism, etching a line of holes through the center of the sign.

The resulting explosion was only slightly less than nuclear. A fireball sprinkled with pieces of truck, bridge, wheels, mushroomed a good forty feet into the air above the river. The clearing smoke revealed nothing but the burning debris of the trailer. The cab had crashed through the metal guard rail and now rested somewhere beneath the rocking surface of the river.

Sergeant Lyle Wallace climbed stiffly down from behind the gun. The Convoy was finally over.

It was the damndest big funeral procession that Albuquerque, or any other city, had ever seen. At its head, the casket, empty since the Duck's body was never found, rode in state on the back of a cabover flatbed truck, the bullet shredded rubber duck from the dredged up cab mounted proudly on the gleaming wood like an emblem.

Behind the lead truck and its motorcycle escort came several undertaker's limousines filled with ex-wives, children, immediate and extended family. Following them were more limousines carrying many who looked suspiciously like politicians, major and minor officials on the way up or the way down. Bringing up the rear was the longest damn convoy of trucks that the world has ever seen outside of a major war zone.

The first several blocks were occupied by heavy-duty cross-country rigs – K-Whoppers, Jimmies, Macks, Fruitliners – washed and polished to a blinding brilliance and rumbling like a procession of leashed animals. Following them was an even longer line of trucks of every age, shape, size and description, from massive earthmovers to laundry delivery wagons. A little boy at the corner by the park began counting the vehicles. When he reached his limit, 100, and there was no end in sight, he gave up and went back to playing with his friends.

On one of the smaller flatbeds a nationally-known folk singing group was introducing what would be its next million seller – a mournful, low-key ballad called 'Goodbye Rubber Duck'. Despite its carnival appearance, the mood of those in the procession and the thousands who lined the streets to witness its passing was uniformly somber. A great man, one of them, had died.

A television newsman from one of the local stations stood in the middle of a group of truckers, talking professionally into a mini cam. "They came in semis, garbage trucks, dump trucks, and even limousines. TRUCKERS. The living embodiment of the American cowboy tradition. A lonely breed. Men too proud to cry, but they can't but shed a tear or two now. The Duck is dead. Who was he? And why does this first martyr of the American trucking industry deserve such respect? For it is love one feels here most of all, the honest love of one man for another that fills this procession and the thousands who have gathered here from all over America to witness this solemn event. And why . . .?"

There was a sudden movement among the circle of men as a massive bearded trucker named Nasty Mike stepped forward and grabbed away the microphone. The camera and sound men scurried around to focus on him.

"I'm tired of this bullshit," he bellowed at the astonished newsman. "And there isn't a man here who doesn't feel the same way." Several growls, whistles and you tell em's from the assembled men urged him on. Nasty suddenly caught the newsman by the collar and began screaming into his terrified face.

"I'll tell you why we loved the Duck. Because of pussies like you, that's why. You government, big business, TV bastards think you own this goddamn country and the rest of us, why we don't count for shit. Ain't that right, boys?"

There was a more menacing growl of assent from the other truckers who had closed up the circle around the two men.

"And," Nasty Mike continued, lifting the newsman up on his tiptoes, "the Duck never took none of that shit. This is our country just as much as anybody else's. And now that he's gone, those sons of bitches blew him away I mean, we ain't going to forget it. That's what this here thing is all about. You tell that to your pussy manager, and your pussy FCC and your pussy government. You tell em that the men in this country are starting to move. And this time they ain't gonna stop us, no way."

He dropped the newsman back on his feet and strode away through the crowd followed by his friends, headed for the nearest bar and one hell of a drunk.

At the edge of the crowd a kind-faced elderly woman turned to a pretty young woman dressed in black with a camera and equipment bag dangling from her shoulders and whispered, "I never heard of him."

The younger woman lowered her camera now that the truckers were out of range and replied simply, "He was the greatest trucker that ever lived."

"Oh, I don't doubt that. I mean judging from the size of the procession here. Are they taking the remains out to Memorial Cemetery?"

Melissa smiled grimly. "No. To Washington. They're

going to put the casket on the steps of the Capitol Building until they get an appropriation to build a permanent monument."

The old lady pondered this answer before speaking again. My goodness, all the way to Washington, the Capitol Building.

"I suppose," she ventured timidly, "he must have been very important. I don't mean to seem ill-informed, but what exactly did he do?"

"He started the convoy," Melissa answered flatly.

"Oh, you mean all those trucks that . . ."

"Yes."

"Oh well, now I understand. It's a shame he had to pass away. Did you ever meet him, this Rubber Duck?"

Melissa nodded.

"Yes. Oh yes, I met him. I was there when it all began."

And in her eyes, the old lady, who was neither quite so naïve or uninformed as she sometimes made herself out to be, could see a story beginning to form.

CHAPTER ONE

IT began one Sunday morning in August on a relatively deserted stretch of Interstate 40 just east of Flagstaff, Arizona.

The week before, Melissa had finished a photo essay on Beverly Hills for Weststyle magazine and a doomed romance with one of its editors within two hours of the same day. The first night she had gone out on the town and gotten loudly, impossibly drunk. The following two days, she brooded. On the third day, she kicked her butt out of bed and picked up the phone.

Within two days her apartment had been sublet and her furniture put in storage. The next day, she dropped the keys in the mailbox and headed out of the City of Angels for good. She had spent a day in Las Vegas, but in her present state of mind, the tinsel and glitter, the unfunny jokes, the whole forced good time of the place had become unbearable. So early that morning just as the sun was beginning to show on the eastern horizon, she had hit the road again.

She didn't quite know what was coming next. Now she was simply driving east with some vague idea of catching a plane in Houston for Rio de Janeiro where she had a friend and a possible assignment for a national magazine. That was one nice aspect of being a photo journalist once you were well enough known. You could work pretty much when and where you wanted to.

Although she was feeling sore and battered, she had lost at love before (she wondered if anyone ever reached the age of thirty-two without such losses) and she knew that in time she'd bounce back. I'm getting a little better, she told herself, a little faster every time.

Up ahead she noticed a large truck in her lane. It was moving out at around 70 m.p.h., which wasn't nearly fast enough for her in her present mood. She floored the accelerator and pulled out to pass. As she edged by the front of the cab she couldn't help but notice its strange hood ornament – a rubber duck. She had a brief, blurred impression of the driver from the corner of her eye – a slightly younger Marlboro man. Interesting.

For the Duck it was another routine haul, Class B explosive chemicals to Indianapolis. He had made the trip enough times that the very real danger of his load didn't disturb him much. It was there, the sense of possible disaster, just like awareness of height when you are walking close to the edge of a cliff, but there was no use brooding about it.

He noticed the yellow XKE convertible and the girl in it as she pulled around him. After the first few hours on the road, there was very little out of the ordinary that escaped your attention. Damn – she was a looker all right. Almost had to be, driving a car like that. He knew Violet would be waiting for him at the Glide Inn about an hour ahead, but it sure didn't hurt to look. Yes sir, she was some kind of rich bitch. He found himself wondering what women like that were really like, how it would be to lay one.

During her passing maneuvers, the chiffon scarf that kept Melissa's hair out of her eyes while she drove had come loose and almost blown away. Once she was safely past the truck she slowed down to forty to retie it, meanwhile steering with her knee.

Behind her, the Duck had to hit his brakes to compensate for her sudden deceleration. Goddamn, what did the dumb broad think she was doing? He laid on the horn a couple of times, but she went on working on the scarf as if there was no one else on the road for a hundred miles in any direction. Muttering most of the obscenities he'd ever come across, the Duck downshifted and pulled out to pass her.

But Melissa was not about to allow that. She'd had enough trouble getting by that damn truck once. Besides, he could wait just a few seconds more. She was almost through with the scarf.

So as the truck pulled up even with her, she accelerated to match his speed. After another quarter mile, the Duck, who had been occupying the opposite lane for the whole distance, goosed it again in an attempt to get by. Again Melissa kept pace with him. She was becoming more than slightly annoyed at the whole thing.

Then began one of those incredible screaming, cursing, hell-bent-for-leather races down the full width of the highway. At the end of a mile, both vehicles were up in the seventy-plus zone, and neither had given an inch to the other. They swept around a curve, bounced through a series of dips. Suddenly, head-on in his lane, the Duck was confronted by a police cruiser, leisurely making its way back toward home base at Flagstaff. Duck saw the horror on the driver's face as he accelerated into the ditch to avoid the collision. Too late for sure, the Duck instantly slowed and pulled behind Melissa, who promptly floored the XKE and began drawing away. Swooping up behind him, the Duck could see the cruiser's flashing lights. Resigned, he began to pull over. Christ, he'd had it this time. The first ticket in six years, and all because of that bitch in the XKE, which as he watched was fast becoming a yellow dot in the distance.

When the officer climbed out of his car, the Duck, who had had run-ins with both cops and policemen before, saw right away that he was dealing with a cop. This was going to be harder than he had thought.

"Log-book, please," the man demanded as he walked up, ticketbook in hand.

"Wait a minute, pardner," the Duck protested. "You've got the wrong vehicle here. The gal in the XKE passed me doin about eighty. Then she slowed down to forty to comb her hair. Then when I tried . . ."

"Your log-book," the cop repeated. He was obviously unimpressed. The Duck handed it over, sizing the man up. He was young, hardnosed, probably just out of the academy.

"Well," he said amiably, "whatever you're writing me up for there, it was damn near worth it."

"What was worth it?" the patrolman's voice was absent-minded, his attention still focused on the information he was transferring to the half-written ticket in his hand.

"The girl in the XKE didn't . . ." the Duck paused long enough for his silence to capture the other man's attention before continuing, "... have any pants on. I took a look and there it was."

The patrolman's official manner was suddenly breached by a flash of uncontrollable lust. Jesus, this was the kind of thing all the oldtimers were always talking about back at the barracks. But all he said was, "Really."

"Swear to God. Belly-button down. Sweetest lookin piece of flesh I ever seen."

"You mean she was just sitting there – naked?" The man was actually beginning to perspire.

The Duck nodded. "Couldn't take my eyes off her, she had to know I was lookin."

"No panties or anything?"

"None." The Duck gazed off into the distance where a tiny yellow dot was about to disappear around a bend in the road. "She's still in sight. You could check it out yourself if you get on it. After all, you got to remember that she was outpacing me in that speeding derby back there."

The man looked hungrily down the road, torn between the half-written ticket in his hand and the promise of forbidden delights. The reflection from the distant yellow dot blinked once and disappeared around the curve. In one continuous movement, the patrolman tore up the ticket, tossed the log book back to the Duck and headed for his car, talking over his shoulder as he ran.

"I'm letting you off with a stern warning this time. But watch your ass from now on, hear. If I catch you speeding again, it's going to be grass – and I'm the lawnmower."

"Yessir," the Duck answered humbly. "You can count on it, sir. You stupid asshole," this last because the patrolman was already peeling down the shoulder of the road in a cloud of dust. The Duck gave him a parting finger as soon as he was almost certain that the distance was too great to recognize it. Grinning triumphantly, he climbed back into his cab and started the engine. As he pulled back onto the highway, he reached for his CB mike and pushed the transmit button. He was back in his world again, and he had a responsibility to fulfil.

"Break one-nine," he spoke into the mike, "for a smokey

report. We got a bear running east on I-4-oh. His twenty is about mile marker two-four-three. Anybody out there got a copy on me?"

"Ten-roger, good buddy," a voice scratched through the speaker. "And we sure do thank you. What's your twenty there, guy?"

"Eastbound about the same spot. Where're you?"

"Bout a mile over your shoulder."

The Duck checked his side view mirror. They were there all right. Looked like at least two of them. "Yeah, I got an eyeball on you," he acknowledged. "Fancy cabover and something behind you there."

"That's a big ten-four, good buddy. You got one Spider Mike from Lubbock, Texas at your back door, and *my* handle is Love Machine. We a Class A truckologist, driving the cleanest Mack machine you have ever seen," the voice went on, managing to expand itself even within the narrow range of the CB transmission. "We call it Love Machine on account of my custom-built orgiastic sleeper cab which comes fully equipped with quadrophonic sound, color TV, pink rabbit fur side paneling, a water bed, bar, and a love mirror on the ceiling, and . . ."

"Yeah and you got something else there, pardner. You got yourself a real motormouth, you ratchet jaw."

"Uh, we take that a little personal there, friend," Love Machine answered carefully. "We hope you got the wherefore to back up that kinda lip. How about it?"

"Now don't get your bowels in an uproar," the Duck soothed, smiling broadly to himself. "Don't you recognize who this is?"

"Negatory. Who this is?"

"This here is the Rubber Duck, you old bandit."

"Hey, Spider Mike. It's Rubber Duck from Albuquerque."

"This the cat that pulled the bars off that Tiajuana slammer for you," Spider Mike drawled back. He had a young voice, slow and gentle.

"One and the same. Walked me home, Duck did. Fed my momma while I was away, too. We got us the best front door in the whole cotton pickin business. Rubber Duck was born with the Smokey Radar. You got a copy on that Spider Mike? Over. How about it?"

"Ten-four. We got you. Glad to be runnin with you, Rubber Duck. My *X-Y-L*'s back at the Home Twenty about to have a baby and we got the hammer down to be there when it commences, 4-10?"

"Yeah, you better be glad, because we're gonna make Ti-i-i-me, boy," Love Machine came back in. "Old Rubber Duck keeps his pedal to the metal and not only that, he don't get caught. The man's bear-proof. How long's it been since you got a ticket, Duck?"

"Oh mercy, been a while now, Praise the Lord, with a real close one already this afternoon. Where you headed, pardner?"

Spider Mike, who turned out to be a shy, likeable blond kid in his early twenties laid back and let the other two men wind the conversation out.

"Atlanta," Love Machine answered grudgingly.

"Atlanta?" Duck's voice was mildy surprised. "What kind of gig you got hauling to Atlanta? That's a new route for you, ain't it?"

"Yeah," Love Machine admitted. "A new job to Atlanta."

"Hauling what? I can't eyeball it from here. You got a reefer on?"

"Uh, negatory. I don't got a reefer on."

The Duck let his rig drift to the left to get a better look back.

"Why, Love Machine," he chuckled, "you ain't haulin go-go girls, are you?"

Spider Mike broke in with, "He sure is. They're closing up my sinuses I can tell you."

Sure enough, on the back of the Love Machine were a hundred of the smelliest, filthiest hogs ever to be shipped from anywhere to anywhere else.

"Don't laugh. Don't you laugh, Duck," Love Machine warned. "I don't see a damn thing funny in this. I mean it."

"I'm not laughing, exactly. I just didn't expect to see you haulin hogs in that rollin whorehouse of yours."

"Well, good buddy. It ain't funny. Mercy sakes it's tragic is what it is. We got us a regular award winning show truck here. Women get hot just lookin at it. And here I am haulin pigs. You tell me, how's my beautiful rig gonna catch me any beaver when I'm haulin smelly pigs?"

"You're going to have to change your handle from Love Machine to Pig Pen for this trip," Spider Mike observed.

"Just a lovin minute there, Mrs. Spider Mike. It took me years to get that handle."

"I don't care how long you been workin at it, *Pig Pen*. All I know is the paint's peelin off my cab, and I'm about to move on by and put you in the back door of this convoy where you belong."

"You gonna have to catch me," Pig Pen squealed. "Hammer down. Gone, bye."

The Duck laughed to himself at the duel for position that he could see forming up in his mirror. He adjusted his speed to stay well ahead of them both. All he needed to make his day complete was a couple of hours tailgating a bunch of hogs.

Pig Pen – somehow the handle seemed to fit his friend, the driver behind him, at least better than Love Machine ever had. He thought back over the years and miles he'd known the other man. Old Pig Pen was a good buddy, but the way he was about that rig of his reminded the Duck of the guy in everybody's high school class who didn't have much to offer the ladies except his magged, superchromed, dual piped, four on the floor, car – and even that never seemed to do him much good. But still he was a good buddy and any company for the long haul on the deserts and plains was more than welcome.

"Hey," he called into the mike, "have either of you seen or heard anything about old Lizard Tongue? I heard he got himself a hair transplant."

"Last time I seen him, he was down in Old Mex' sitting in a pulque bar, and he didn't seem as though he was hurtin none either," Pig Pen answered.

Their conversation was suddenly interrupted by a new voice from up ahead. "Breaker one-nine, this is the Cotton Mouth here, calling the Duck. Looks like I got your front door about the 350 marker."

"I got a copy on you, Cotton Mouth," the Duck answered. "I'm at 343, and I'm needin a bear report."

"There ain't a bear in sight. She's clean and green. Bring it on up."

"Well, front door Cotton Mouth, it looks like you got me and two others in your rockin chair. We'll be coming on."

"Ten-four. That's definitely my pleasure, but you want to convoy with me, you better be a mover, cause this old boy don't know but one way to ride, and that's with the *hammer down*."

"Ten-Roger, Cotton Mouth," the Duck continued the conversation. "What are you pushing there – a 747?"

"Next to those pingers of yours, that's what it might seem like. This ole Jimmy can blow the doors off anything on the road."

"Breaker, breaker," Pig Pen interrupted. "Exceptin maybe my Custom Mark Two Bulldog."

"What's *your* handle?" Cotton Mouth asked with just the trace of an electronic sneer.

"We got the Love Machine here and we driving the meanest, mightiest Mack this here Super Slab ever eyeballed."

Suddenly the Cotton Mouth struck. "Well, the way I hear it," he drawled, "Bulldogs is pussy, pussy."

That did it, for Pig Pen the last straw on an already bummer trip. "Well, I'll tell you what, Mr. Cotton Mouth," he began with exaggerated politeness, "We'll just see about that. We gonna do it, right here and now. And before you can say – *GMC* Jimmy stands for General Mass of Crap, my Bulldog is gonna be nippin the fur offa your raggedy ass. Down and out."

Pig Pen pulled the big Mack out into the second lane and really screwed it down. In front of and behind him, the Duck and Spider Mike went along for the ride. As they roared around the curve ahead, the only vehicle in view was an obscure white Plymouth traveling at about the legal speed limit in the far right lane.

Inside it and praying that those three dumbasses wouldn't notice the CB antenna on his trunk for a few seconds more sat the scourge of I-40, a figure cursed and dreaded throughout the annals of Southwest trucking – Sgt. Lyle Wallace of the Natosha County Sheriff's Department. Lyle busted more truckers in an average week than any other law officer in the state would be likely to corral in a couple of months. He had come to feel that he owned this particular stretch of I-40 and in a way, in the days before the Great Convoy, he did.

He picked up his mike and gave the final call to the slaughter. "Breaker one nine. Cotton Mouth to Rubber Duck and Love Machine. What's your Twenty? I backed it off, down near pulled over here, but I can't see nothin behind me but slab. Mercy sakes, I thought you boys were movers."

Muttering to himself – Goddamningnorantsonsabitch – Pig Pen put the pedal to the metal. More curious and amused since it wasn't their fight, Spider Mike and the Duck kept pace with him.

When they were well within range, Lyle allowed himself one final prod. "Get it on, you turkeys. Where are you?"

A sixth sense tripped in the Duck's head – too late. That Plymouth. As they roared up on it, he made out the CB antenna on the trunk. "Back em down," he yelled hopelessly into the mike. "Back em down. We got a bear in a plain brown wrapper."

Before they could decelerate to anything near the legal speed limit, Lyle had stuck the portable flasher on his rooftop, flipped on his siren and was signaling them over to the shoulder. Leaning his two hundred mostly solid pounds against the car as he waited for the three drivers to come up to him, Lyle was a good-looking man, a lawman who looked a little like an old West sheriff in his Stetson hat and Western cut uniform. The corners of his mouth curled up in a slow grin. Three at once – a really nice score.

When the three men walked up, Lyle took the lead. "Nice day. Screwin it down a bit, weren't you, boys?"

"Hello, Lyle," the Duck answered quietly.

By now Lyle was the image of amiability, practically bursting with good humor. He even reached out and shook the Duck's hand.

"Why howdy, Rubber Duck," he crowed. "Fancy meeting you here. It's been a long time."

"Six years. I should've figured it was you on the two-way."

Now Lyle became concerned, confused, the picture of innocence. "What two-way you talking about?"

"The CB, Cotton Mouth."

"Couldn't've been me," Lyle protested. "I don't even have a CB. Besides, do I look like the kind of man who'd resort to police entrapment?"

"Yeah and a cottonmouth don't look like a snake either, you sonovabitch." Pig Pen's too long suppressed anger spewed the words out more as a gurgle than a statement.

The Duck gave Pig Pen a look that silenced him. "Cool it," he said. "No use making it any worse."

"Yeah, let's keep it civil." Lyle spoke with some relief. He retook command of the situation. "Now I could write you up for seventy-five, but just to avoid unnecessary arguments, let's say you were doing seventy, which will run you about . . ."

"Thirty-five bucks plus another hundred or so for what it does to our insurance," Spider Mike snapped.

Lyle screwed up his face as if in serious thought. "Well," he allowed, "it could be worse than that. You see the judge's wife is going through the change, and he's been on the wagon . . ."

"How much?" the Duck interrupted. He was already reaching for his wallet, only too happy to escape without the mark.

"Oh, let's say fifty each."

"You are one low scummy mother." Pig Pen's voice began as a growl and ended at a roar.

Lyle looked at him calmly. "Sixty," he said.

The Duck grabbed Pig Pen's arm and pulled him back a step or two. "Take it easy," he cautioned. "This ain't no auction."

"It's a punk beef. Cuts all the profits out of my trip," Pig Pen sputtered.

"That wipes me out," Spider Mike chimed in. "I don't have enough money for food."

"Well, if you'd rather take your chances in court," Lyle began reasonably, "I've got a real nice jail. And I'll impound your rigs all nice safe while . . ."

"Got to hand it to you, Lyle," the Duck broke in as he forked over the fifty. "You're the biggest goddamn pirate on the road and you get away with it."

Pig Pen and Spider Mike passed over their money. Spider Mikes's was in singles, fives and tens. Lyle counted it all carefully and tucked the bills into his shirt pocket.

"Just doin my job," he said cheerfully. "Keepin the highway safe."

Spider Mike's eyes were riveted to the wad of money in Lyle's pocket. His money. What about his wife? And the baby that was just days, maybe even hours away from being born?

"Yeah chump," he snarled at Lyle. "Maybe someday you'll find yourself keeping the highway safe off in a ditch somewhere feeding flies."

Lyle looked thoughtfully at Spider Mike. "For you, it's seventy."

"Come on." The Duck stepped between the two men, facing Spider Mike. "Don't make it worse on yourself. I'll pay him the extra ten now. You give it back your next trip, okay?"

"Bullshit." Spider Mike was still plenty mad, swinging mad.

The Duck seized both of his shoulders and shook him. "How'd you like to be doin time when that baby is born? Would you like that?"

After a brief hesitation, Spider Mike shook his head. The Duck released his shoulders and smiled. "Then cool it," he said softly. "Let me handle this."

"By the way, Lyle," he continued as he handed the money over, "I understand you're going to be one of us soon."

"How's that," Lyle asked, on his guard but curious.

"Teamsters are organizing the cops, I hear."

"Not this cop. I wouldn't be part of your damn union if you paid me."

"Not mine, Lyle," the Duck replied calmly. "I'm still independent."

"Well, at least we have one thing in common." As he had when they had walked up, Lyle extended his hand. The Duck simply stared at it until it dropped back down.

"Two," he said flatly looking Lyle straight in the eyes. "We hate each other." The obvious, simple truth of the statement cut through the surrounding bullshit and reduced all of them to an uncomfortable silence. Finally Lyle cleared his throat and gave them what was intended to be a jaunty smile. He turned abruptly and slid into his car.

"Just goes to show. You can't please everybody."

The Duck walked over and looked down at him.

"You please me, Lyle," he said softly. "I can't tell you how much you please me. I just hope that someday when you're not wearing that uniform, I'll get the chance to show you how much you please me."

For a moment Lyle tried to hold his stare. Then he turned his attention to starting the car. He started to say something, floored the accelerator instead and roared away, spinning a blinder shower of dust and pebbles over the men behind.

Pig Pen watched the Plymouth out of sight. "That sure is one cold mother." His voice was balanced on the edge of a cool rage. "One day him and me is gonna meet, and it ain't gonna be beside no highway in broad daylight neither."

The Duck put a hand on his shoulder to steer him back toward the rigs.

"A lot of men have said that over the years. It ain't happened yet. Come on, let's roll our butts out of here. We already wasted a half hour of good daylight on this bull pucky."

A minute later they were back on the road thundering toward Rafael's Glide Inn and at least a decent meal among their own kind.

And that, although nobody could know it at the time, was the way the Convoy began.

CHAPTER TWO

RAFAEL's Glide Inn was acknowledged among the regular I-40 truckers as the only choke 'n' puke worth stopping for between Flagstaff and Albuquerque. Up until the end of the fifties, it had been a sleepy two-pump gas station and diner that depended on the desert heat and its isolated location for the few customers that trickled in on their way to somewhere else.

Then one day, a trucker named Monihan got a little too high, forgot to pay attention to his rpm's and burned a sleeve right in front of the station.

As he sat most of the day in the shade behind the pumps waiting for the tow truck from Flagstaff and watching the rigs – mostly cross-country haulers – pass by, an idea was forming in his mind.

It started as a simple – "Shit, I'm gettin tired of hauling my ass all over this country for peanuts. A man my age (it was 46) ought to get into something a little more substantial." Then his hemorrhoids began smarting, he'd already had two operations and was well on his way to the third. So, he sat and thought some more. Then when the tow truck finally arrived, he rode into town, sold his rig and bought the station cash on the barrelhead.

His first move was to replace the gas pumps with diesel. Then with the last of his cash, he built an extension on the back of the diner, which he divided into a shower room, TV room and novelty shop full of cheap goodies to send to the wife, the girlfriend, the kids back home. As a concession to the local trade, he retained the original name, *Rafaels*; the addition of *Glide Inn* was solely his, an idea that came to him the night that his first customer had swooped in off the highway and rolled up to the pumps. He was off the road for good, but he was making a place for his own.

His latest innovation had been the installation of a CB radio in the Call-In section of the restaurant so that he could simultaneously keep track of potential customers in his area and, not incidentally, accept their orders to be ready on arrival.

This particular afternoon, Thelma, the older of the waitresses, was handling the CB call-ins. Almost painfully drab and plain, Thelma was the kind of person who, were she not actually working at the Inn, would have been discovered by Hollywood to play such parts on the screen. But she was conscientious and good-hearted in her limited way, and everybody liked her.

Liked her even more, oddly enough, than her younger co-worker, Violet. Violet had the kind of lush, sultry allure that drives men mad at eighteen and disappears at thirty. She was twenty-one now and only beginning to fade like a just overripe fruit still swaying on the topmost bough. She was the darling of the company, and probably the source of more midnight masturbations along the length of I-40 than a man would care to count. But everybody knew she was the Duck's girl whenever he came through. The Duck was the best and Violet had a very clear idea of what she deserved.

So the men who passed through once, twice, three times a month, the quiet ones with their gentle talk and set eyes that seemed to see miles beyond you, desired Violet, respected the Duck and each other man to man – and everybody liked Thelma. It was not the worst of arrangements or places on the road to be.

Violet was slouched down against the counter idly eavesdropping on a mildy diverting conversation between Widow Woman, a black lady trucker who had outlived four husbands on the road, and the expensive looking girl whose yellow foreign convertible had just been towed into the garage dripping oil all over the place. Still the girl didn't seem too upset. That was what money could do for you.

Violet fell into her favorite daydream – of herself, cool, calm, gracious dispensing her favors to the great and the near great on the patio of her Beverly Hills estate. No, she would never forget the little people, no matter how high she rose. A well-known voice on the CB snatched her back to reality.

"Breaker one-nine calling the Glide. This here's the Duck. E.T.A. three minutes."

"Anything you want, Duck?" Thelma asked innocently.

"Thelma," the voice cackled back, "you always ask me that. What's the matter, wasn't last night good enough?"

Thelma blushed. That was one of the reasons why everybody liked her.

"Oh, by the way, Thel, would you tell Violet that I'm running late because of a little Smokey problem and I'd like to get my order right away. She'll know what that means."

"Jesus," Widow Woman commented to Melissa, "anybody in the world who isn't dead from the waist down can understand what *that* means."

"And that's the guy you said I ought to hitch a ride to Albuquerque with?" Melissa demanded suspiciously.

The Widow Woman spoke with a seriousness that could only have come from the heart, or very close to it.

"Honey, do you see these?" She was pointing to a row of four badges running neatly down the bib of her overalls like a column of campaign ribbons.

"Each one of these is for one of my four husbands." She fingered the first thoughtfully. "This one was my first husband. I started driving with him when I was seventeen."

"What happened to him?"

The Widow Woman smiled at the eagerness of Melissa's question. This girl hadn't really had the chance to get close to life yet, but she was alive. Widow Woman liked people like that.

"He got in a fight, they shot his ass," she answered casually and went right on. "Then came the Red Gallo. He was Italian, he only lasted one summer. Then, Julian, he drank too much. He was the father of my kids, liver blew on him." She touched the final badge. "Then old George here."

"Did he die, too?" Melissa was getting a little concerned as the story went on.

"Uh, huh. But he died happy." Widow Woman chuckled happily and slapped herself on the knees. "But you listen to me, honey," she continued, all the time holding Melissa's eyes with the strength of her own. "I've known some men in my time. Real men – not those two-bit punks they keep turning out nowadays that'll sell you out for a nickel and go runnin home to Mommy when the road gets rough. And I'm here to tell you that the Duck is a real man, the kind of man you can count on no matter what. That's why I said you should ax him for a ride to Albuquerque. I'd ride anywhere in the world with that man, and sleep like a baby the whole way."

"He's trouble." The intense nasal voice of Violet ripped open the envelope of their conversation like a knife.

The Widow Woman looked up at Violet in disgust. "To you, anybody's trouble. You wouldn't know what to do with a real man if he tripped over you."

"You lyin bitch," Violet spat back. "You're just jealous because you're old."

"Honey, I ain't ever gonna *be* as old as you *are* right now."

"Hey, the Duck's here," somebody called out, and sure enough there was the familiar black Mack easing into the lot followed closely by Pig Pen and Spider Mike. With a little squeal of dismay, Violet gave up the battle and headed on the run toward the Ladies Lounge.

"I gather she's his girlfriend," Melissa remarked, amused.

The Widow Woman humphed out the last of her anger and said, "That's what *she'd* like to think. Actually she's just a half hour stop he makes going to and from."

"To and from where?"

The Widow Woman winked.

"From everywhere else."

The two women burst in helpless, hysterical laughter just as the Duck walked through the front door. Thinking that he might be their object and a little nettled that the girl in the XKE he'd just seen being towed into the garage was part of it, he walked over to Widow Woman and demanded half goodnaturedly, "Hey, Widow Woman, you ain't laughin at the old Duck here, are you?"

"Of course we were, darlin," the Widow Woman choked out, her eyes still wet with tears of laughter. "Didn't anybody ever tell you how really ugly you are?"

"A man don't meet that many totally blind people on the road these days," he answered suavely. "Tell me, how come you ain't picked out that husband number five yet?"

"I already have, darlin. I'm just waitin' for you to grow up a little and notice what you been missin. Set your butt down and buy us a beer."

"Since you beg me, okay."

He took the empty stool next to Melissa and nodded to her amiably as if she were a casual acquaintance he hadn't seen for some time.

"What happened to your car?" he asked. "I saw it in the garage."

"Oh, I was just driving along – nude as usual – and it threw a rod."

The Duck laughed. "The cop caught up with you then."

Melissa nodded. "Thanks a lot," she said. "I can appreciate a little bullshit from an arresting officer. Livens up my day."

"Exactly how much bullshit we talkin about here?"

Melissa shrugged. "I sent him to the motel of his choice. He's probably still waiting."

"And then she called old Uncle Lyle," the Widow Woman put in.

"Who seemed very interested in your big black truck," Melissa added.

"And got me my first bust in six years," the Duck concluded for them both.

"Yeah," Violet came back sarcastically, "I suppose you were having a race."

The Duck and Melissa looked at each other and broke out laughing, which made Violet even more furious. And gave the Widow Woman the opening she'd been looking for.

"Duck, we was hopin that is I suggested to Melissa here that since her car is shot and she's missed the last bus East until mornin that maybe you'd give her a ride into Albuquerque so's she can catch a plane."

The Duck was about to shake his head no as soon as he found a suitable explanation when Violet wedged her way back into the conversation and changed his mind.

"Nice girls don't ride in trucks," she snapped at Melissa.

Then she turned to the Duck. "If you take her with you, you're asking for trouble."

The Duck smiled a frigid warning at her. "I wasn't intendin to, but you make it sound so interesting that I'm not so sure anymore."

"What do you say then, Duck?" the Widow Woman urged.

'I'll tell you later," he said, taking the three women in with his glance. He stood up and focused on Violet. "Let's go," he said curtly. "I'm runnin late."

"Sure, Duck, sure." Violet draped her apron over the sink and stepped through the opening in the counter by the cash register. "After all, it is your birthday."

It was a running joke between them. They had first made it on the Duck's birthday over a year ago, and now every time he managed to stop by was his birthday and Violet was in charge of his present. On this particular occasion, he was horny enough to be interested, but he was definitely not amused. He walked out of the building ahead of her. She caught up about halfway across the parking lot and took his arm.

"You aren't taking that bitch anywhere, are you," she said, halfway between a demand and a question.

The Duck removed her hand from his arm before answering. "The more you tell me not to, the closer I come to doin it. I told you a hundred times, keep your claws offa me."

Violet decided to pout. "You've got no heart," she sulked. It was a line she'd heard the night before on an old TV movie, where it had produced excellent results for Linda Darnell.

But Linda Darnell hadn't been dealing with the Duck. "I'll tell you what else I ain't got," he said deliberately. "I ain't got a husband doin ten to thirty in the slammer for armed robbery."

Violet moved closer and lowered her voice to silence him. "I told you not to ever mention that around here," she hissed. "I've got my reputation to think about."

The Duck snorted his answer to that.

"Besides, Charlie wasn't so bad. He just had some hard luck," she continued.

"Yeah, and I'm looking at the worst of it. The way I heard it, he was tryin' to bust that bank to take you to Hollywood. Any truth in that rumor?"

"If there was, at least he cared enough about me to *do* something to get me out of this hellhole."

They had reached the Duck's truck and were standing just outside the cab door.

"Listen," he said, "I'm tired of all this jawin. You want to shut up and get it on – or not? It's your choice."

Violet was in a bind. Everybody knew what she and the Duck were out here for. If she went back in now, she'd be a laughingstock. Besides, she'd been with him long enough to know that if she left, he'd just make it up with that rich bitch, who was plenty more than willing whether she knew it yet or not, and drive off with her.

Violet reached a decision. She had a reputation and a territory to protect. She'd get even on Mr. High and Mighty Rubber Duck another time, maybe cut him off some night when he was really horny and there was nobody else but Thelma around. She opened the door and climbed into the cab with the Duck right behind her.

Inside the sleeper, she let him undress her. She was wearing her Happy Birthday bra, that she had lettered in red fingernail polish just after they had met. But her real surprise was underneath – a pair of red pasties that she'd cut into the shape of hearts with her nipples sticking through the notches. When he got a load of those, they'd see who had the upper hand with who.

Meanwhile back in the restaurant, Pig Pen and Spider Mike had come in from the shower room just as Violet and the Duck were leaving out the front. They walked over and sat down on either side of Melissa and Widow Woman.

"Where's he goin," Pig Pen asked the Widow Woman, indicating the departing form of the Duck with a backward jerk of his thumb.

"Collecting his birthday present," she answered wrily.

Spider Mike leaned over and kissed her on the cheek. "Hey, Widow Woman," he said softly.

She gave his hand a squeeze. "Hey, Spider Mike. It's good to see ya."

"My handle's Love Machine," came Pig Pen's voice from the other end of the quartet. He had naturally taken the seat by Melissa.

"Not hardly," Spider Mike declared. "This trip it's Pig Pen." To the Widow Woman he added, "He's haulin go-go girls."

"That's temporary," Pig Pen answered, unruffled. He turned back to Melissa. "As I was sayin, my handle's Love Machine, and I hear you're lookin for a ride. If so, I got the cleanest Mack Machine you ever seen . . ."

"This lady already has a ride – with the Duck, Pig Pen," the Widow Woman cut in.

"Well, in that case," Pig Pen said, his mind obviously shifting gears at a phenomenal rate, "I'll just take her bags out to his rig for her."

The Widow Woman kept a step ahead. "Later, Pig Pen," she snapped knowingly. "I'm sure that the Duck will be happy to see your *big nose* out there with them bags – later." She turned to Melissa, effectively sealing him out of the conversation. "You married, honey?"

"Not any more. Not for a few years."

"Got tired of that barefoot in the kitchen shit, huh?"

Melissa sensed that however unlikely it might seem in the social circles she usually traveled with, she had found a friend – another woman who cared.

"I certainly did," she answered. "It was more than that. It was . . ." She spread her hands to indicate the years of heartaches, hopes, disappointments, realizations that lay behind her. The Widow Woman nodded.

"I hear where you're coming from," she assured the younger woman.

Pig Pen said, "Excuse me," and stretched over Sam for the sugar. On his way back, he asked, "You from around here?"

"Who me?" 'My God,' thought Melissa looking around, 'anything but that.'

"Hey, Pig Pen, look out there."

Pig Pen spun around, following Spider Mike's voice and pointing finger to see Lyle just pulling into the parking lot in the unmarked Plymouth. He began cruising slowly along the circle of parked trucks.

"What do ya suppose he's doin?" Spider Mike wondered aloud.

"Checking plates, I imagine," the Widow Woman suggested.

As he stared sourly at the CB antenna on Lyle's trunk, Pig Pen had an idea. He tapped Spider Mike on the arm and led him up to the CB at the call-in window. He took the mike from Thelma and spoke quietly into it.

"Breaker, quick. You read me?" Then he handed the mike to his partner and whispered, "Say yes."

"I read you," Spider Mike replied more or less automatically. "Whattaya want?"

Pig Pen took the mike back and said, "We got a bear cruising the lot checking plates. You got all this year's tags?" He shook his head at Spider Mike indicating the answer he wanted. Spider Mike reached for the mike. He was beginning to get the idea.

"Negatory," he said with real despair. "I'm screwed. He's gonna get me sure."

"Well, jump out. I got some hot ones. Slap them on and he'll never know."

By this time everybody in the restaurant and pool room, where the CB was piped in, was beginning to catch on. Pig Pen and Spider Mike shut off the mike and went to join the crowd of hysterical men at the windows.

Lyle had pulled his car in at the far end of the line of parked trucks and was getting out. Stealthily, in the best approved Indian manner, he began working his way back on foot, using the beds and boxes as cover like trees in a forest. His method of attack was to pussyfoot around the tailgate of each rig and pounce – on nothing. Several of the men in the cafe were laughing so hard they had to sit down.

Out in the sleeper, the Duck and Violet had been resting between rounds when the conversation began on the CB, which Duck always kept on whenever he was in the cab on the time-tested theory that the more you knew about what was going on the better off you were. One of Violet's pasties was dangling off the end of her breast. The other had disappeared completely.

"That's old Pig Pen," the Duck said. "And that's Spider Mike. What do you suppose they're up to?"

Violet didn't know or care. She draped an arm high up on the Duck's thigh to distract him. But at the first mention of the cop in the lot, the Duck began pulling on his pants.

"Where you going, honey?" Violet demanded petulantly.

He brushed her aside as he reached for his shirt. "I got to get an eyeball on what's goin on out there. Might be trouble."

"Well, if you've got to . . ." Violet stretched full length in the sleeper pushing her breasts out toward him like twin invitations.

The Duck's glance passed right over her and he went back to pulling on his socks. "I got to," he said.

As he levered himself out of the sleeper, Violet grabbed his arm. "Well, I'm just not going to let you go," she declared in her best Scarlett O'Hara manner. Unfortunately her tug caught him off balance and pulled him bodily back into the sleeper, cracking his head solidly against the rear wall. It was the last goddamn straw.

"I told you to keep your claws off me," he bellowed. "Now I want you to get your clothes on and move your ass out of this truck – for permanent."

"But, Duck, I was only playin."

"Bullshit. This whole thing between you and me has been a bum trip since the beginnin. We ain't for each other, except like this, and you know it 's well as I do. Well, I'm endin it here and now."

He crawled up into the cab just in time to witness a truly extraordinary sight in his side mirror. Lyle Wheeler came suddenly bounding around the end of his box, hand on gun and ready for bear. When he found the lane between the two parked trucks empty, his face fell for a brief moment, and then he began sneaking with comic caution around the tail of the next rig in line.

Lyle couldn't figure it out. From what he'd overheard on the CB, he had an easy bust right under his nose. He was already past the point that he had been checking from the car on his way into the lot, and he still hadn't found a thing out of line. Maybe if he tried the radio again, he'd get some further clue. Keeping close to the line of trucks, he sprinted back to his car.

As soon as he saw what Lyle was up to, Pig Pen dragged Spider Mike back to the CB in the café. The other drivers gathered around. This was going to be fun. Pig Pen put a finger to his lips to silence them and opened the mike.

"You got em on, Charley?" he said in the same tense whisper he'd used before.

"I do, and I sure do thank you," Spider Mike answered. "That old Smokey's gonna have to sniff up his own butt for a while."

"You know who that bear was? Old Dirty Lyle. Ain't he an overweight mother, though?"

"The word is *fat*, man."

Now they were off. Pig Pen took his turn with glee. "Wait till he gets out of his car and see how he bounces around out there." He finished with a low suggestive whistle.

"You mean he's one of them semi-beavers I heard about?"

"Yeah. Like one of them hairdressers you see around, y'know."

Lyle had begun cruising very slowly back toward the café, checking each of the cabs for the source of this damned transmission. He cringed when he remembered that it was going out for at least thirty miles in every direction.

"Hey, that's probably why's he's going around collecting all that money – to have one of them sex change operations. The next time we see him, he'll be all pussy."

A couple of the men in the audience broke up at that and had to be hustled to the far side of the room before they gave the whole scene away. Outside, Lyle was nearing the café end of the parking lot. Part of the group headed for the windows to watch the expression on his face.

"I don't think he's human." Pig Pen began again. "He's kinda like some slimy, crawly reptile, you know. Kind of like a snake when ya come right down to it."

Something clicked in Lyle's mind. That voice.

"Well, whatever he is, pardner, when the Good Lord was passin out assholes, Old Dirty Lyle sure came back for seconds."

That did it. The whole room dissolved in laughter just as

Lyle noticed the CB antenna on the roof of the café and put two and two together. His gaze traveled down the building to the front windows, where he found a whole café full of truckers watching and laughing their asses off. Sons of bitches. He floored the Plymouth and squealed to a halt by the front door. Somebody, and he had a pretty good idea who, was going to get his ass busted for this.

He burst into the café like a bullet and headed straight for Spider Mike.

"Duck," Thelma whispered into the CB in the sudden stillness, "you better get in here. It looks like trouble."

The Duck was already pulling on his second boot when the message came. Back in the sleeper Violet was buttoning up her blouse.

"I gotta go," he said, holding the cab door open for her.

"Do you mind if I get dressed first? Could you take the time for that?"

"Nope." He slammed the door shut and went on talking through the window. "When I get back, that sleeper better be empty, understand?"

"You bet I understand." Her eyes, which had been streaming tears began filling with the fury that Hell hath none like. "You're riding pretty high and mighty, *Mr.* Rubber Duck. But somebody's gonna bring you down one day. And I'm gonna be there to dance on your grave, you son of a bitch."

By the time the Duck reached the café, Lyle's plan of attack had reached phase II. He had shoved Spider Mike up against the bar and was in the process of busting him for vagrancy. The Duck pushed his way through the crowd to the two men.

"Sorry about the trouble, Lyle," he said casually. "We'll be hittin the road." He took Spider Mike's arm and started toward the door.

"Now just a damn minute," Lyle protested.

"He's busting me for vagrancy," Spider Mike broke in. "And I'm not going to any slammer, man. My old lady's having a baby and I'm going home."

"It's true, Lyle. His wife is nine months and two weeks gone," Pig Pen put in from the crowd.

"Anybody know who the father is?" Lyle sneered. He turned back to Spider Mike. "Get back up there, you."

In the far corner of the room, Melissa was edging toward the door and outside. Whoever's fight this turned out to be, it clearly wasn't hers. All she wanted was a ride to Albuquerque. Tomorrow at this time, she could be in Rio de Janeiro sipping margaritas and watching the sunset over the bay.

Lyle grabbed Spider Mike's arm and tried to push him back against the counter – which led him straight into the right cross that knocked him on his ass. For a moment he lay there, stunned, fumbling instinctively for the service revolver on his belt. He was dimly aware of the Duck holding the kid off above him. Then just as he had the .44 out and ready to put a hole in the young punk, he heard the Widow Woman yell, "Duck, watch out for the piece," and before he could get the revolver aimed, the Duck's feet spun toward him. There was a flash of boot headed for his jaw, and then the lights went out for good.

"Get out to your rig and haul ass," the Duck ordered in the stunned silence that had set in.

Spider Mike stood looking down at Lyle's unconscious body. "It appears to me that you'd better get to yours," he said softly.

Pig Pen stepped out of the crowd. "You two gonna flap your jaws all day, or are we gonna roll it?"

The Duck dragged Lyle over to the counter and locked him to the footrail with his own handcuffs. Then he handed the keys to Thelma.

"Keep an eye on these. You can find them outside about an hour after we're gon, okay?"

"It's a privilege." Thelma dropped the key-ring in the pocket of her uniform.

"Oh, and, uh, sorry bout this." The Duck walked over to the café CB and yanked the microphone off. "We'll pay for it the next time through."

Thelma nodded. The Duck looked over at Pig Pen and Spider Mike. "Let's haul ass."

As they started for the door, someone in the back of the crowd began to applaud. The clapping and cheering was picked up by others until the whole room was shaking with it. In the confusion Violet slipped up to the Duck by the door.

"Take me with you," she begged. "I got to get out of this hole."

He shook off her hand. "Are you kiddin? This ain't no milk run, baby, and if it was, I mean what I said out there a while ago. You and me's through."

Her fingernails clawed at his arm, leaving three long red marks from elbow to wrist. "Then go to hell," she screamed. "You just go to hell."

Outside the Widow Woman came up as they were marching across the lot. "Where you headed, Duck?" she asked.

"We got to take it to the limit, I guess. Which means gettin into New Mexico the fastest way."

She turned toward her truck. "Well, let's go."

"Hey I thought you was headin South."

"I am, sort of, but me and a couple of the boys," she pointed to two rigs that were already fired up with tiny puffs of smoke rising from their exhausts, "well, we figured you might use some company."

"I'm mighty obliged, Widow Woman, but I don't want to take you out of your way."

She gave him a wink. "When you get as old as I am, the only reason you take a way is so's somebody can come along and pull you out of it. Let's haul our asses out of here. Old Lyle ain't gonna stay out forever."

Within a minute, the six trucks had pulled out of the lot, heading east toward New Mexico and relative immunity to an Arizona pursuit. As usual, the Duck took the front door, while Spider Mike tended the back. Behind the Duck was Widow Woman, followed by Nasty Mike and Dapper Dan, the two new recruits who were hauling furniture to Louisiana. Then came Pig Pen in the Love Machine. As soon as they got up speed, the Duck put the hammer down. There was no way to go back, nothing to go back for. The run to the border was on.

Back in the café, Violet had just poured a glass of cold water over Lyle. He still lay flat out on the floor, sputtering and trying to shake some of the fuzz out of his head. The first thing to take his attention was the fact that he was handcuffed to the counter footrail with his own handcuffs. With a groggily muttered, "What the hell?" he pulled himself to his knees and began patting his pockets for the key, which of course wasn't there.

"All right," he growled up at Violet and Thelma, the only two people left in the place, "who in hell took my keys?"

"Keys? What kind of keys?" Thelma asked. Violet said nothing, just stood there staring down at him with a queer look on her face.

"The handcuff keys, you dumb bitch!"

Thelma turned delicately away. "I don't think there's any call to use that kind of language," she said demurely.

"Thelma, give him the key." Violet's voice was a tightly controlled monotone.

"Why, Violet, I don't know at all what you mean."

"We both know that you have that key," Violet said in the same flat voice. "Give it to him."

"I will not. You know what the Duck said."

Violet walked over to the cash register and took the protection revolver from the shelf beneath it.

"Now. Give him that key or I'll blow you away, so help me God." The barrel was pointed squarely at Thelma's chest.

"You wouldn't have the nerve," she gasped, thinking maybe she would.

"Wouldn't I? I'm assisting a police officer in the performance of his duty. I imagine I wouldn't get off too heavy on that rap, eh Lyle?"

"You get me that key, and I'll guarantee you self-defence." He wasn't too sure why Violet was doing this, but he was on her side.

"Thelma." Violet's finger tightened just perceptibly on the trigger. "I'll do it if I have to. *Now give him the key.*"

Mechanically, like a poorly animated mannikin, Thelma walked over to Lyle and dropped the key ring in his lap. He scrabbled around furiously, getting in his own way several times before he finally freed himself. Before he bolted to the door, he took a last look at Violet.

"Jesus, you must hate him a lot," he said.

She smiled at him with a bitterness that he'd seen before only in the faces of the lifers at the state prison. "Enough," she said in that strange emotionless voice that seemed to have become a part of her.

After Lyle had disappeared through the front door, Thelma walked over to Violet and slapped her once, hard. The sound rang out in the stillness like a shot.

"You'll rot in hell for this," she hissed.

Violet began laughing. She laughed and laughed. "I'm already in hell. And I'm fixing to get myself a bunch of company."

CHAPTER THREE

GETTING free of the cuffs was only the beginning of Lyle's troubles. He almost ran down the battery in the Plymouth before he thought to check the distributor cap, which had been thoughtfully removed by Pig Pen on the way out. Lyle had already noticed that his CB antenna had been torn from the trunk of the car. Grand theft, he thought. Good. That was another rap they'd have to answer for. With any luck, before this thing was through, he could probably get all three of those bastards for five to fifteen, easy.

He rushed back into the café. Thelma was standing by the call-in window, dangling the severed CB mike from her hand like a yoyo. She smiled at his entrance.

"Nice try, Lyle. You know, I had a feeling we hadn't seen the last of you."

The phone, he knew, had been out of order since the night before. He dashed back outside and scanned the parking lot, which turned out to be occupied only by three semis at the far end. Even if he could commandeer one of them, there would be no way to overtake those rigs with another one just like them. He had to do something now. If those bastards made it over the New Mexico border, he'd have a hell of a time getting at them. Commandeer. Maybe that was an idea. Sure enough. Out of the heat mirages that were just beginning to form in the distance, he could make out a car coming his way. He stepped out into the highway and raised his arms.

"Jesus Christ, he's pulling us over. Gimme that baggie." In the car approaching Lyle, Roger Staggers – 17, blond, skinny, pimply-faced, and his current girlfriend Sammantha Egbert – 16, equally blond and skinny although not so pimpled, had been out blowing grass to pass a peaceful Sunday morning. In the baggie she handed him was a little over an ounce of primo homegrown marijuana. Needless to say, they were more than a little struck by Lyle's sudden appearance.

Suiting action to situation, Roger emptied a little over half of the contents of the baggie into his mouth, handed it back to Sammantha, indicating with grunts and gestures that she should do likewise with the remainder. When she was equally apple-cheeked, he lit the almost empty baggie with his lighter and was just able to shove the crumpled burning mass into the ashtray by the time the car reached Lyle.

"Police officer," Lyle said curtly. "I'm commandeering your vehicle. Get out, both of you."

"Ou wha?" Roger garbled.

"Listen, dummy. I want that car." Lyle threw open the door and yanked Roger out on the highway. "You'll get it back, tomorrow." Lyle assured the two of them. "Call the sheriff substation in Haroldsburg."

"Mma, uff." Roger was keeping his head turned away to hide the dribbles of homegrown he could feel at the corners of his mouth. Under the circumstances, he was relieved to be only losing the car.

"You know, buddy, you got quite a speech problem there," Lyle observed as he ran through the pedals and gears. "Maybe you ought to see somebody about it."

When he was gone, the two teenagers looked at each other and began to giggle. Spurts and then showers of slightly masticated marijuana came flying from their mouths.

Out on the highway, Lyle eased the sixty-eight Galaxie up to fifty and then floored it to see what it would do. The resulting acceleration jammed him back in his seat. Jesus, the kid must have some kind of plant under that hood. He watched in fascinated disbelief as the speedometer needle broke a hundred smoothly, still climbing. Lyle screwed it down and sat back smiling. He wouldn't even need the kid's CB. With this baby he could overtake those bastards in half an hour at the most and make the collars himself. He could already see the headlines:

TRUCKERS ASSAULT OFFICER
MASS ARRESTS NEAR NEW MEXICO BORDER

Thirty minutes later and forty-five miles down the road, the convoy was, as usual, jawing on the CB.

"Pig Pen to Rubber Duck. What do you think, pardner?"

"I think we got us a *convoy*, old buddy."

"Duck, this is Spider Mike. Look, I'm sorry for getting you into all this. I shouldn't of hit him."

"Well, if you didn'ta, then we wouldna had a chance to bust his ass," the Duck allowed. "You see him catch that foot. Whooeow!"

"Yeah, I believe you rattled his cage real good," the Widow Woman added with a chuckle.

"Listen," the Duck said, "everybody get a copy on me. I got us a little secret route across the state line, bout forty miles ahead."

"Once we cross that, think we're okay?" Spider Mike asked.

"Maybe," Pig Pen broke back into the conversation. "But don't count on coming through this state again for a while. There'll be piles of warrants all over the place."

"Believe me, coming back through here is about the last thing I'm aiming to do," Spider Mike declared. "Hey, Duck, what about that big agricultural check station at the border? You got a way around that, too?"

"I think so. Let me check the map. Over and out."

The Duck hung up his mike and began rummaging through the glove compartment. After running over everything in the box twice and not finding the map he wanted, he remembered that it was probably somewhere up in the sleeper behind him. Keeping his eyes on the road, he twisted his arm around and began feeling for it with his fingers.

While all this was going on, Lyle had caught and passed the rest of the convoy and was bearing down on the Duck's rig at something over a hundred miles per hour.

Just as Lyle pulled up even with the rear of his box, the Duck found something in his sleeper. It was definitely not what he expected. It was soft, warm under the fabric that covered it. It felt almost like a tit. It was a tit. His mind momentarily blown, the Duck let his truck swerve to the left:

Almost sideswiping Lyle, who was within seconds of passing him;

Causing Lyle to make a too sharp cut to the left to avoid the collision;

And setting up a most spectacular exit by Lyle from the roadway altogether.

The Duck heard the CB scream, "Smokey in plain wrapper on your left," and glanced out of his window in time to see Lyle's car strike the embankment beside the road and set off on a fantastic flight. It ripped through a TAKE A FRIEND TO CHURCH billboard on the way up, soared twenty more feet and crashed squarely on the roof of a hay barn, which caved in neatly like a studio prop, leaving Lyle, scared well beyond shitless but physically unharmed, on top of a ten foot pile of bales.

"Godalmighty," the Duck breathed to himself, all thoughts of who his mysterious passenger might be driven momentarily from his mind. He thought he had made out a CB antenna on the back of Lyle's car before it had disappeared into the barn. He reached for his mike. The convoy had slowed to a fraction of its former speed almost like tourists viewing a wreck.

"Rubber Duck to Lyle," the Duke called hesitantly, not at all sure of what kind of answer to expect. "Got your ears on there, good buddy?"

"Yeah, I can hear you," Lyle answered after a few nervous seconds.

"You okay?" the Duck asked. "Need a meat wagon or something?"

"No, I'm just fine, Duck. Fine." Now that the shock had been wearing off, Lyle was more mad than hurt.

"Well, I'm glad to hear it. You know, you were beginning to grow on me, sort of like athlete's foot once you've had it long enough. Keeps you moving."

"Yeah, well listen here, butterass. The charges on you and your buddies just went up from felony assault one count to felony assault three counts, plus escape, plus false imprisonment . . ."

"Plus wreckless driving," a feminine voice came from Duck's sleeper. By God it was the snooty broad from the Glide Inn. "Conspiracy to felonious assault," the voice continued fatalistically, "assault with a deadly truck. Technically it's kidnaping – not false imprisonment. I did a series on the criminal court system once."

"I see you got your girlfriend with you," Lyle came on spitefully. "Well, the same goes for her, too."

"Honest to God, Lyle," the Duck protested in her defense," I didn't even know she was there until just a minute ago. As a matter of fact, you might say that discovery is why you're sitting back there in that barn right now."

"Ten years," Lyle countered. "I figure it at about ten years with a little time off for good behavior."

"Yeah, but you're forgettin one thing, old hoss. You got to catch us first."

"I got the state police in on this right now." Already Lyle's voice seemed to be getting a little fainter. "You read me? Lyle Wallace and the state police are gonna lunch your ass."

"Well, lotsa luck, Lyle. See you in New Mexico. If you ever get by Albuquerque, be sure and drop in."

The Duck hung up the mike and half-pulled, half-guided Melissa into the cab seat. "Buckle up," he ordered, pointing to the passenger lap belt. "We are gonna move."

Ten minutes later, three highway patrol cars came screaming up to Lyle, who had made it to the side of the road beneath the ruined billboard. The first car pulled over to let him hop in.

Lyle slammed the door and offered his hand. "Lyle Wallace. Natosha County Sheriff's Office. Man, am I glad to see you."

The patrolman shook his hand, noting without comment the handcuff dangling from it. "Bob Bookman," he said. "Glad to be here. I hate those fuckin truckers."

Meanwhile the Duck had found his map and his bearings, and was speaking into the CB.

". . . bout ten miles more. It's a right turn onto a gravel road. Just keep your eye on me."

Beside him, Melissa shifted uncomfortably and loosened her seat belt. "Look, I've been thinking this thing over," she began. "And maybe I should get out somewhere along here. I think I could hitch a ride quite easily." The Duck frowned at her here, but she decided not to pay any attention. "So, if you'll just pull over," she continued, "I'll get my things out of the back."

She reached into the sleeper and pulled her suitcase down

onto the seat. The Duck continued concentrating on the road, ignoring her. When he hadn't slowed in a couple of miles, she said, "Ready," in a much too cheerful voice.

"For what?" the Duck asked, his eyes still searching for the cutoff ahead.

"To get out."

He looked at her briefly then. "You want out?" he said. "Okay."

Without slowing he reached across her and opened the cab door. Then he began nudging her toward the blur of the road that was flashing backward at between eighty and eighty-five miles per hour. Melissa screamed. After a few seconds, he reclosed the door.

"Listen, lady, we've got a bunch of bum raps chasing us back there, and our one chance is to make the New Mexico border before Lyle and his buddies catch up, or throw a roadblock on us. I didn't ask you here. When we get across the border, if we get across the border, then we'll talk about letting you out. If you want out now – jump."

"I'm sorry," she said after a moment of thought. "When you wouldn't stop back there, I guess I panicked."

"Happens to everybody one time or another."

"I just didn't want you to add the Mann Act to your list of charges."

"Mann Act? That's for under 18-year-olds."

Melissa shook her head. "It also covers the transportation of a nervous woman across state lines for illicit purposes."

The Duck broke into his first real laugh for a long time.

"Take a valium," he advised. "Here we go."

He decreased his speed slightly and pulled a sudden right onto a dirt and gravel road that angled off across the desert to the infinity of the horizon. As if they were connected, the five trailing trucks swung onto the road behind him with no noticeable loss of speed.

There were six trucks in the convoy, all of them eighteen wheelers. Six times eighteen equals one hundred and eight wheels all kicking up gravel, rock and dust from the roadbed. A huge cloud of dust began to rise.

Looking back at it, Melissa commented, "The perfect escape route. They'll never guess we're here."

The Duck put the pedal to the metal. "If we make it to that pass up there, it don't make a damn what they guess."

Back on the highway, Lyle suddenly yelled, "There she blows. It's just what I told ya. They're taking off on a secondary to by-pass the border station." His finger indicated an almost mushroom-shaped cloud of dust on the horizon.

Bookman allowed himself a grim smile. "If that's as far as they are, we got em dead." He slowed a bit looking for the intersection, found it and pulled onto the secondary, followed closely by the other two cars. The two lead cars raised an immediate dust cloud that made driving almost impossible for Patrolman John Duncan who was bringing up the rear. He turned on his windshield wipers to see if that would help, it didn't. Then he began to sneeze.

Up ahead the trucks had moved two abreast, a maneuver that reduced their dust problems but created a blinding fog for the cars behind. When they reached this residue from the trucks ahead, Duncan was a lost man. He bounced through a dip and missed the curve at the top. The cruiser flew off the road, ripped out a ten foot section of barbed wire fence, demolished a fledgling yucca, rolled twice down an arroyo and came to rest on its side in the dry stream bed. After the dust had cleared, the front door swung open, and a dazed but basically unhurt Patrolman crawled out. His lips were moving to the words of a childhood prayer.

Back on the road, the battle raged on. Sgt. Price in the second car ran into a savage fit of coughing that forced him to pull over, out of the action.

But Lyle and Bookman were made of sterner stuff. Both were holding handkerchiefs over their faces in a futile attempt to fight the dust that enveloped them like a shroud. Lyle's free arm was crooked around the stock of the riot gun.

"Faster," he coughed. "We got to git close."

Bookman swerved sharply to avoid the ditch. "Goddamnit," he snarled, "if you think you can do any better, you're welcome to drive."

Only half-hearing Bookman's reply, Lyle peered ahead, searching the shifting gray curtain of dust for any sign of the vehicles creating it. They must be getting close.

Up ahead, the Duck had problems of his own. His heat

gauge had been up in the red for the past couple of minutes. He couldn't keep up this pace much longer. Pig Pen's voice sounded over the CB.

"Pig Pen, I mean Love Machine, to Duck. How far we got to go, Duck?"

"I was hoping you could tell me."

"This ain't exactly what my rig was built for," Pig Pen complained. "I mean I'm worried about my waterbed busting. She ain't had this much shaking since I caught them twin sisters in Carlsbad."

Melissa suddenly broke out in a deep joyful laugh.

"What's with you?" the Duck asked, puzzled.

"I'm a Radcliffe girl," she answered laughing even harder.

The Duck didn't get the joke. Was she freaking out? He wouldn't blame her if she was. They broke into a stretch of oiled road, and her laughter stopped as quickly as it had begun. The dust-free rear view revealed the police car less than a length behind Spider Mike who was running a solo backdoor again.

Lyle and Bookman made their move. First they tried passing on the left, and Spider Mike almost put them through the fence that lined the road. Then they tried the right, but again he swerved, sending them halfway up the embankment where they teetered dangerously on two tires until they finally pulled down to level again with a teeth-shaking jolt. While they were recovering from that, he moved up in the left lane and began running side by side with Pig Pen, effectively blocking any further attempts to pass on either side.

Pig Pen looked out his window and waved. "Hi ya, Spider Mike," he called cheerfully on the CB. "Hear tell we got some bodacious bears behind us."

"Do tell. Well, let's widen up here and have a look."

Still running side by side, the two trucks split apart, opening up a lane between it. It was Lyle's golden opportunity. "Go for it!" he screamed, pounding Bookman on the shoulder and pointing to the open lane between the trucks. Bookman goosed the cruiser and then pulled up between the two boxes. When it was well inside, Pig Pen called again.

"I don't see any bears, do you, Spider Mike?"

"No. I don't see nothin. Might as well close her up."

"Okay, on three. One, two, *three*."

Bookman and Lyle had only a terrified moment to realize what was happening before the two trailers swerved back together, pinching the car between them in a perfect squeeze. The results were immediate and catastrophic. The doors, side windows and front fenders of the car were instantaneously annihilated. Blue smoke rose from the front tires, which blew out within seconds of each other, fishtailing the car to inglorious defeat.

For a long moment, Lyle and Bookman simply sat in the wreckage and watched the last of convoy disappearing over the next rise. When they were gone, Bookman leaned over to Lyle and said distinctly, "Puppy shit."

Lyle sprang into action. He punched the radio, which turned out to be out of action. He pushed, wedged and finally kicked open the bashed in door on his side of the car.

"Come on," he called to Bookman. "Get your ass in gear. We got to find the other guys – and a radio that works."

Bookman had had enough. "What for? the border's not five miles ahead. They'll make it sure."

Lyle's mouth contorted in a smile of more than normal hate. "From where I'm sittin' that's going to be their problem. We ain't through yet."

Melissa had time for one more valium before they passed a crude hand-lettered sign that said "Welcome to New Mexico". About a mile later, the convoy turned onto the highway and headed east. The Duck began singing, and the rest of the convoy joined in via the CB, "Jingle bells . . . jingle bells . . . jingle all the way."

Suddenly he gave Melissa a grin and blasted his air horn. The full-throated bass roar, closer to a train than an automobile horn, started her upright in the seat. From back in the convoy, Pig Pen answered. Then all six of the trucks were blasting away. It was the loudest damn noise Melissa had ever heard and it went on for almost a minute, by the end of which she was shrieking and yelling with the others. They had made it. Together they had come through.

When the horns began subsiding, the Duck yelled into the CB.

"Whooee, you boys are something else. How you doing?"

"Just doin a job," Spider Mike answered. "That right, Pig?"

"That's right, *boy*, and the handle is Love Machine. Hold on."

Pig Pen had spotted a convoy of three trucks and a chartreuse van idling at a crossroads ahead.

"Breaker, breaker, one-nine," he called. "This is the Love Machine lookin for them rigs on the side up there. Got a copy on me?"

In the lead rig was the Bald Eagle, a veteran of uncountable miles whose days behind the wheel went all the way back to the labor troubles in the late forties. He was a stocky little man whose head, as his handle suggested, was completely without hair beneath the leather beret that he took off only to sleep.

"Ten-roger. We gotcha, Love Machine," he answered in an alert, raspy voice.

"Whattaya doin sittin there?" Pig Pen asked.

"Waitin for you. We heard you modulatin the last half hour, so we know all that's gone on. And we definitely want to give you all congratulations on a job well done."

"We sure do thank you." Most of the convoy was past the side road now.

"Ten-four. And if it'd be all right with you, the Sneaky Snake, Buffalo Bill, and this here is the Bald Eagle – we'd be real proud to be part of your convoy."

"And don't forget us . . ." came a voice from the van.

"For sure. For sure," Pig Pen answered them both. "Just slip em in the back."

"Heay, we got a buncha long-haired friends of Jesus here," Buffalo Bob noticed in his mirrors. "You fellas go ahead. I'd just as soon handle the back door if it's all the same with you."

"Why certainly, brother. Certainly," answered the voice from the van, which had HONK IF YOU'RE GOING TO HEAVEN painted across both sides in flaming letters. "You got the Reverend Joshua Duncan Sloan of the Church of the Wayfaring Strangers here, and I don't read nothing in the scripture that says, 'Thou shalt not put the pedal to the metal'."

"And that's a truth," Pig Pen came on. "Reverend Sloan, you just slide in the side there. We definitely happy to have God on our side."

The Duck turned the CB volume down on the chatter between the convoy and the new recruits.

"Are you on the road all the time? I mean . . ." Melissa asked.

"Right now I am. I like to keep moving." The Duck gave her a quick glance, sizing her up. "It appears to me you're somethin in the same boat."

Melissa tossed back her hair. "For now I am," she admitted. "Someday I'll settle down."

The Duck chuckled softly to himself. "That's what I used to think."

They began to pass rigs idling beside the highway or stacked up by twos and threes at the major crossroads. Pig Pen had assumed the role of the official Welcome Wagon and was kept busy directing the new arrivals into the back door.

The convoy swelled to twelve, then fifteen, then seventeen vehicles pounding down the road. Mostly they were big interstate rigs, but there was one short hauler with ADAMS PEANUT BUTTER stencilled proudly on his box. Behind him was a bright gold-leaf painted truck with black scrolled lettering across the tank that proclaimed: SEPTIC SAM YOUR SEWER MAN – YOU DUMP IT WE PUMP IT.

Melissa stuck her head out the window to check the size of the convoy. She was amazed. "Unbelievable. I've never seen anything like it. What are they doing? Where are they all coming from?"

The Duck shrugged. "Don't ask me – ask them. I'm just a poor boy lookin for Big Indy."

"Where?"

"Indianapolis. So's I can drop that can back there. Then I'll make myself scarce for a while."

"But what about those other trucks?"

"Them? You could say they're my cover. They'll split when the time comes."

Melissa frowned. It all made sense, but there seemed to be something missing. The Duck decided to lead her on a little.

"Look, it's just a convoy . . . only this's a little bigger than most. One way to beat the bear."

"You're not going to tell me that this is just a game," Melissa flashed back indignantly.

"Not exactly," the Duck explained. "To a trucker miles is money. When you come right down to it, it's all hangin on the most miles in the shortest time. Now old Smokey has got a license to steal. He's got the double nickel, ah . . . five-five speed limit, and the ICC. He's got the scales, the radar, and the rule books. Nothin easier than to hang paper on a trucker – and he don't often turn out to be the mayor's nephew."

"All right," Melissa conceded doubtfully, and then moved on to the question she really wanted to ask. "But why are all those trucks out there following *you*?"

"How do I know? Probably as many reasons as there are trucks out there," the Duck answered philosophically. Then sensing that she was still lost, he continued, "Look, when I drive, I just drive. Lotta gearjammers, they're thinking about anything but. Got their minds on baseball or pussy or they're writing poems in their heads or woolgatherin about what they're gonna do when they're ninety-nine. And then there's Dudes who go out lookin for trouble. Maybe they like a flare with the bear once in a while, who knows? Me– I'm a cautious son of a bitch."

"You? Cautious? We're felons. We're fugitives going ninety miles an hour down a dead end road, and you tell me you're cautious?"

The Duck looked at her seriously. "Back there, I did what I had to do and that's what I been doing ever since. You really want to know why those trucks are lined up back there? Because I'm a concentrator, that's why. I think about my road, my speed and my chances. And when I got that all worked out the best way I can, and not before, I say Hammer Down."

Melissa looked at him thoughtfully. "Full Bore," she said softly.

"What?"

"I had an uncle who used to say that. I think he meant pretty much what you mean by Hammer Down."

"What happened to him?"

"He was flying his own plane from Phoenix to Acapulco a year ago last March and he just vanished. The crash site was never found. He was sixty-eight. I loved him."

"Everybody buys it sooner or later," the Duck said gently. "I guess it's not when but how that matters."

"That's funny. That's what he used to say when we'd tell him he was getting too old to fly."

They flashed past a sign that said: OFFICIAL WEIGH STATION – ALL TRUCKS MUST STOP, and then were upon the station itself, a small building on a rise in the middle of a quarter-mile asphalt turnout. As they reached the turnout, the Duck jammed the accelerator and roared on by, and the rest of the convoy followed suit.

Inside the weigh shack, Officer Elfont Jeeter was bored. He was dividing his attention between a three-month old *Playboy* he'd read at least twice and idly keeping an eye on the passing traffic when suddenly a big black Mack semi with some kind of funny hood ornament tooled right on by without even slowing down. Then came another, and another, and another. Godalmighty, there must be upwards of twenty altogether, all screwin it down like the devil himself was tailgaiting them. His first impulse was to run for the patrol car behind the shack. Then he remembered all those trucks flying by like a weighmaster's nightmare, and headed for the radio instead.

Back down the road in Gallup, Special Agent James Hamilton was called away from his barbecue by an official phone call. He came in wiping barbecue sauce off his hands and hoping this would be something that could be handled tomorrow morning.

"Jim, this is Roberts down at Division. We've got a little trouble in your area, and we hoped you could handle it."

Hamilton winced at the "we". It usually meant a nasty job with not even anybody particular to bitch to.

"What's up?"

"Well it's a little out of the ordinary. According to the reports we have here, it seems that a bunch of truckers ganged up on an Arizona sheriff, left him handcuffed in a truck stop and let out for the New Mexico border. After demolishing two police vehicles, they crossed the border about an hour ago heading East. Since then, they picked up some others and now they've got a convoy traveling hell bent for leather straight across the state. The latest report is that they buzzed right on by a weigh station near Bridgerton."

Hamilton took off his barbecue apron and draped it over a nearby chair. "What do you want me to do?" he asked resignedly.

"I've already put Charlie Fish on this as a backup. He'll be arriving at the airport in a half hour in a copter to pick you up. He'll have the Arizona officer, a ... a ..." Roberts shuffled some papers "... Sgt. Lyle Wallace with him. We're going to put you down in Allington. The local chief of police has already been notified of your arrival and he's promised full cooperation. You should have plenty of time to set up some kind of roadblock, nip this thing in the bud before it gets any more out of hand. One of the wire services has already picked the story up. Any questions?"

"Only one. Who's the leader of this convoy."

"All we have for now is his CB name – Rubber Duck. We'll try to have more for you by the time you reach Allington."

"Okay. Will do."

"Fine. And Jim, this kind of thing has a way of snowballing sometimes. The Bureau wants it stopped, and stopped hard. Do whatever you have to."

Hamilton mumbled goodbye and replaced the receiver. "Elaine," he called through the patio door, "you'll have to finish the steaks. And forget about mine. I've got another special." Jesus Christ, he thought, what a way to spend a Sunday.

Back in the Duck's cab, Melissa was nodding out under the combined effects of all the excitement and the three valiums she'd taken in the last two hours. Over the turned down CB, the voice of Pig Pen could be heard.

"We got the Rubber Duck for our front door. You all come on in."

The count was now up to over twenty rigs of various sizes and descriptions, and still growing with every mile.

CHAPTER FOUR

"FANTASTIC. Simply unbelievable," Hamilton breathed, mostly to himself.

The convoy had expanded to twenty-three vehicles, over half of them long haul diesel semis, all of them speeding along at the 80 m.p.h. pace being set by the Duck. The helicopter raced the length of the column and settled in a groove above the big black Mack. It was time to begin phase two of Hamilton's plan.

The trip to Allington had gone smoothly enough. On the way, Lyle had filled the two FBI men in on the situation. Hamilton's private opinion was that the man was an unmitigated ass, but his career so far with the Bureau had convinced him that emergencies often made strange bedfellows so he decided to hold his place for the time being. Chief Stacy Love and two of his men were waiting for them by the helipad atop the Allington central police station.

In the squad room, they had set up an enlarged detail map of the county. One of the patrolmen, who was either Bart or Barry, stepped up to it and began explaining.

"Right now they are located approximately here," he said, pointing to a spot on the far left of the map.

"That's about fifty miles West?" Hamilton asked after a quick check of the scale.

"Yessir. About that."

"Between there and here is mostly farmland," Fish observed, studying the topographical features closely. Bart nodded.

"Is it a good area for a roadblock?" Fish went on.

"Over here would be better." Bart was pointing to a spot about five miles west of town. "We can get our men out there quicker and there's some rock ledges that come up to the road on either side that make a natural barrier in case they should try to go around."

Fish looked to his partner for confirmation. Hamilton nodded.

"Sure, looks fine," he agreed. "How many trucks are there now?"

"About sixteen last count," Lyle broke in, "but the sons of bitches are like flies on shit. More keep a'comin."

'Jesus,' Hamilton thought, 'with Sheriffs like these, who needs criminals?' Aloud, he addressed himself to Chief Love.

"Get as many men out there as you can and start setting up the barricade. A double row of cars across both lanes, reinforced by timber should do it. We're in contact with a judge in Santa Fé and should have the telephone authorization for a warrant in what?" He turned to Fish. "Twenty minutes?"

"About that," Fish confirmed.

"Agent Fish and I will take the copter and intercept the convoy. We'll do what we can to stop this thing before it gets started. But if we fail, I want that block ready and waiting for them."

Chief Love turned to the two patrolmen. "Go get the men together," he ordered. "Barry, you get on the squawk box to the Sheriff's and the Highway Patrol. We're in need of every man we can get. Bart, I want Campbell and Bob Clark in on this, too."

As the two FBI men headed for the exit to the helipad, Lyle tagged along. He caught up with them on the roof.

"I thought I ought to go along with you fellas," he said. "After all, I was the original arresting officer."

"Yes. Well things got a bit carried away, didn't they?" Hamilton replied with more than possible sarcasm.

Lyle was stung. "You think some desk jockey could have handled it better?" he demanded.

Hamilton shrugged resignedly and made room for Lyle in the copter.

"Maybe not. But this is the first time since I've been with the Bureau that we've been called out to enforce a simple speeding violation."

He had signaled to the pilot so that whatever Lyle might

have said was lost forever in the chattering roar of the rotors.

And here they were hovering over the convoy itself. Getting a grip on his distaste, Hamilton turned to Lyle.

"Are they all in communication with each other over these citizens bandradios?" he asked.

Lyle nodded. "Right."

Hamilton tapped the pilot on the shoulder. "Is there any way I could speak to them on their radio?" he asked.

"Sure. What are they on, channel nineteen?"

"Right," Lyle confirmed again. He was beginning to enjoy being the resident expert.

"Attention all trucks! Attention all trucks." In his official, public role Hamilton spoke with a resonant authority that was a little surprising if you had talked with him privately. "This is Special Agent Hamilton of the FBI. You are ordered to stop your vehicles immediately. I repeat. Stop your vehicles immediately. You are traveling in violation of Federal Law."

There was not the slightest response from the convoy. Lyle began feeling a little more smug. Those truckers would never answer. The guy couldn't speak their language. Hamilton, however, was not about to give up.

"Attention, driver . . ." he checked a crumpled report in his hand,' ". . . Martin Penwald."

"Who?" Lyle blurted in real puzzlement.

"Their leader, Penwald," Hamilton explained in a quick aside. "Attention, driver Martin Penwald," he repeated emphasizing each syllable of the name. "Do you read me?"

Again there was no answer. Lyle decided that this old turkey shit had gone far enough.

"You're doing it wrong," he advised with a condescending patience. "Just say Rubber Duck – you got a copy on me?"

"Rubber Duck?" Hamilton asked, slightly confused. He knew he'd heard that name somewhere before.

"Yes. That's his CB handle. He won't answer to anything else," Lyle explained. "Go ahead."

"Well . . ." Hamilton gave it a last valiant try. "Attention, driver Rubber Duck. Stop your vehicle at once. You are under arrest."

When there was still no answer, Hamilton sat dangling the

mike from his hand. "Maybe they didn't hear me," he said without much hope.

Lyle swung into action. He put out his hand for the microphone, and Hamilton passed it over.

"Break one-nine. Break one-nine," Lyle called with just a touch more expertise than was absolutely necessary. "This is the bear in the air, Officer Lyle Wallace calling Rubber Jerk in that rattling piece of black crap at your front door. Come on."

There was a long enough delay for Hamilton to reflect that he wasn't really sure which side he would have been on in that café back in Arizona. Suddenly, surprising them all, the Duck's voice came on.

"Please don't be using that kind of language on the air, Lyle," he drawled innocently. "And especially don't be using it in regard to my beautiful black truck."

"That thing you call a truck is the sorriest pile of garbage I ever had the misfortune to write a citation on," Lyle sputtered. "And Duck," he went on in a cat-and-canary voice, "take a look on up the road there, fella. We got us a roadblock up there with twenty armed men, and they all got orders to shoot you and that black turd full of holes 'less you pull over."

"For the third time, I'm asking you not to talk that way about my rig, Lyle." In the Duck's voice was that calm, overly patient tone a parent uses with a troublesome child. The effect was not entirely lost on Lyle.

"You can shove that dog piece of tin, Rubber Jerk," he screamed, losing all control of himself and his voice.

Down in the truck, Melissa was getting scared. She looked over at the Duck questioningly. He didn't seem overly concerned. He winked at her and began to speak.

"Okay, Lyle. Tell you what. I want you to do something for me – go up there and personally stand on that roadblock. But before you do, take a look at the sign on the side of my trailer."

Hamilton leaned over the window jamb, but could see nothing except the top of the box. He signaled the pilot to drop lower.

"See em?" the Duck continued when he was sure they'd

had a good look. "Chemicals, it says. That's explosive, Lyle. Nitro-mannite Class B explosives. Now I'm not sure of the difference between class B and class A explosives because I never had call to test it out before, but I have a feeling that 'less those boys on the roadblock get outta my way real quick, they're gonna be sitting up on clouds eating angel food cake. Rubber Duck. We gone. Bye."

He switched off the radio. Melissa stared at him with horror-filled eyes.

"It's not really explosive?" she cried hopefully.

He nodded, contradicting her.

"But you're not just going to crash into the roadblock," she said a bit more desperately.

"Unless they git it out of the way, I am."

"You're kidding."

This time the Duck answered with the accelerator. Rrrrummmm. No, he wasn't kidding. He was crazy, this whole thing had been insane from the start. How could she ever have thought otherwise? The Duck continued to accelerate – eighty, eighty-five. Melissa sat back wondering idly which way she was most likely to die. She realised that she must be in shock, but all the valium in the world wouldn't help her now.

Up in the chopper, Lyle was doing his best to reassure the two agents.

"He's just bluffing," he said confidently. "Believe me, I know the man. He'd never do it in a . . ."

"You want to be responsible for all those lives?" Hamilton snapped. He checked the convoy again. It was within five miles of the barricade and moving faster than he liked to think about. He shook the pilot's shoulder urgently. "Call the roadblock," he ordered. "Tell them to get the hell out of there."

The command from the copter struck among the men on the ground like an incoming mortar. At first they scattered in all directions and had to be reassembled to remove timbers and double line of cars stretched across the road. As they worked feverishly, they could hear the rumble of the convoy's engines coming closer beyond the curve that they had hoped to use as camouflage. They were still struggling with the last of the cars when the Duck roared around the bend full throttle and bore down on them.

Most of the men dove for cover, but two of them, whose bravery above and beyond the call of duty went virtually unnoticed in the ensuing events, managed to maneuver the final car far enough out of the way that the Duck's bumper merely clipped its back fender, sending it spinning off into the ditch.

Victory! They were through. Right behind the Duck came Widow Woman smiling and waving at the shaken police. A few trucks later, Pig Pen went through, his middle finger rigidly raised in greeting.

When the last vehicle was safely through and disappearing into the distance, Chief Love allowed himself to sag back and wipe the sweat from his forehead and eyes. Jesus, that was a close one for sure. Now all he and his men could do was get back to TOWN.

He began racing to his car calling out wildly to the other officers, who were mostly trying to cope with the post-adrenalin shakes.

"My God. They're headed right for town!"

The race began. The police vehicles took to the shoulder to pass the convoy which had slowed momentarily to celebrate its triumph. With sirens flashing and full advertising on, the Chief's car, which was being driven by Bart, roared past the Duck and began the race to town. The Chief was on the radio to all units.

"I want all traffic, everything stopped. Get somebody there to wave them through. I want traffic control at every signal. And for God's sake, get your butts in gear. You've got about two minutes before we hit the West End."

Melissa was scared to death and breathing as if she'd just run a couple of miles at least. The Duck chuckled a maniacal little laugh in her direction, inviting her to join in.

"Jesus Christ," she screamed over the noise of the motor which was running flat out as the truck began to gain on the police cars ahead. "You're out of your mind."

He nodded, smiled to show her that he knew it, and chuckled again. There was something elemental about the sound as if it welled up from the very center of his life.

'He'll be laughing like that the day he dies,' Melissa thought. 'I just hope this isn't it.'

The Battle of the Gargantuas, which was the Sunday Spectacular movie being carried by the locally owned and operated TV station, KTNM, was interrupted by a newsflash. It was delivered by Dennis Pavlone, who wrote, edited, announced and sometimes fabricated news for the station.

"Up date! Emergency!" he came on in his best Tom Brokaw manner. "We have just received word that the runaway convoy of trucks that we told you about on an earlier bulletin has broken through the roadblock that was set for them in the Parsons Corners area and is headed for downtown Allington at this very moment. The latest available information indicates that the lead truck, which is being driven by a man known thus far only as the Rubber Duck, may be carrying volatile chemicals. The police department warns all citizens to stay off the streets. If you are presently driving within the city of Allington, pull over to the curb immediately and await further instructions. We're taking our mini-cam unit to the scene, and if you don't hear a loud explosion in the next fifteen minutes you'll hear from us. And now we return you to our Sunday Afternoon Spectacular, *The Battle of the Gargantuas*."

Undeterred by the unscheduled break in the action, the bad Gargantua went back to tromping on an airfield while the good Gargantua kept clobbering him with a high voltage telephone tower.

Outside in the city of Allington, things were not quite so calm. Traffic had been moving normally along Main Street for a Sunday afternoon, when suddenly the distant sounds of police sirens sent the vehicles scrambling for the nearest curb, where they waited as they usually would for an ambulance or fire truck to pass. All of a sudden a motorcycle cop appeared going like sixty down the middle of the street and screaming at the waiting cars to pull even further back. Nobody really had time to figure out what all that meant, or do anything about even if they had, before the convoy was upon them, moving at a good seventy-five miles per hour.

To the six-car police escort and the trucks following, the street, checkerboarded with cars and pedestrians, resembled a high speed obstacle course in an arcade. Bart, a man much more talented than Chief Love had previously guessed, led a fantastic motorized hula dance through the center of town. The procession wove in and out of the banks of parked cars, onto the wrong side of the street, through intersections against the lights.

What pedestrians were about had been warned well in advance by the approaching bedlam and lined the curb wondering what the hell was going on. What they were treated to was still the craziest damn thing they'd ever seen – a million damn trucks speeding right down Main Street with a police escort. Not a few of them wondered if national security might not be involved, but even the most diehard of these were hard put to account for the Peanut Butter truck and Septic Sam according to that theory. When the Church of the Wayfaring Stranger passed through with the Reverend Sloan, as he had promised, keeping the pedal to the metal, most of them gave up even trying to guess and headed home to see what the evening news would have to say.

The convoy burst through the central business district and started heading out the East Side. The Duck was laughing like crazy, having the time of his life. Melissa didn't know whether to scream or cry or laugh or whatever else. She had the distinct impression of being caught in the jaws of a monster, but also that there was something she hadn't previously suspected to be said for it.

The Duck was checking the trucks behind him in the side-view mirror.

"Will you look at that," he said wonderingly. "Did you ever in your life see so many trucks?"

He started laughing again, this time with a deeper, heartier sound. Listening to him, Melissa knew what he meant. Although it scared her, she too could feel the power of the convoy, power enough to make a dent in things, at least for a while.

"Why are we doing this?" she asked breathlessly as they raced through the outskirts of town toward the open highway beyond.

The Duck scratched his head. "Damned if I know," he confessed. "We started out just tryin to keep a skip and a jump ahead of old Lyle." He paused and took another look in the mirror. "But I reckon all that's changed now. It's kinda like a snowball rollin downhill."

"You know they'll get you sooner or later." She hated to be a prophet of doom, but some things had to be faced.

To her surprise, the Duck laughed aloud. "Yeah," he conceded, "but I'm used to it. I've had that same feeling for some several years now."

They rode for maybe a mile in silence except for the chatter on the CB, which had become too crowded with conversations to be really comprehensible. Then Melissa came back to the point that had been sticking in the back of her mind like a burr.

"I guess I can see why you and Pig Pen and Spider Mike are doing what you're doing, but what about those other drivers out there? They're not running from the law. Some of them are probably going hundreds of miles out of their way. What's with them?"

The Duck took a while to think that through before answering.

"I don't know for sure, but if they're thinkin like I am, maybe I can give you a clue."

She nodded him on and sat back to listen.

"It's like this," he continued. "A person like you, you've lived most of your life on the topside of things or I miss my guess." She nodded again. He was right of course, but it wasn't her fault. What did he want her to do – be poor on purpose?

"Well me and most of those people out there," he went on, "we've been looking at things from the underbelly most every day of our lives. And one thing you catch on to right quick at the bottom of the pile is that although everybody's supposed to be born equal in this country, there's some people that have their minds set on takin up all the room.

"This here convoy," he concluded, indicating it with a sweep of his hand toward the mirror, "is maybe our way of sayin we're here, too. And we got to be counted a little more often."

"Well," Melissa shrugged, "I guess there's nothing else to do."

"Than what?" the Duck asked cautiously.

Suddenly she gave him a crazy, infectious grin to match his own.

"Hammer Down," she said.

Back in Allington, Hamilton was on the police radio to area headquarters.

"He said he was carrying explosives. . . What? You checked the manifest and he *is* carrying nitro-mannite." He paused to give Lyle an accusing glance. Manfully resisting the temptation to present the other man with the well known bird, Lyle turned and stared out the window for the remainder of the telephone conversation.

"Yes, it does change things," Hamilton continued. "In my opinion this is no longer a situation that can be handled by local enforcement agencies . . . what, the governor. When? Water skiing! A fine goddamn thing at a time like this. Okay, I'll stand by. Over and out."

"The National Guard," Lyle breathed with satisfaction. "Rubber Duck, we are surely gonna lunch your ass."

"You know what, Wallace?" Hamilton commented as he and Fish headed for the twenty-four hour greasy spoon next door to the station. "If we do get another roadblock out of this, I'm going to personally see that you're assigned to stand on the top of it."

This time Lyle did give him the finger.

"Age or IQ?" Hamilton snapped, reverting instinctively to the eighth grade level from which he was being attacked.

"You'll find out," Lyle stormed. "I don't need you uppity sonsabitches, or the Governor to handle one lousy gear-jammer and a bunch of his asshole friends. I got me a plan, and it don't include you."

"Thank God for that," Hamilton replied in kind. "Being around you makes me much too sympathetic toward the other side."

The slamming day room door concluded the conversation between them, but in the world outside, the wheels went on turning, rolling them all toward the final, inevitable climax of what had been begun back in the Arizona desert so few and yet so many hours before.

CHAPTER FIVE

About fifty miles further east from their location at the end of last chapter, the convoy was on the verge of discovering that there are more animals than bears prowling the roads. It began with what looked like a snake rising up outside the window of the Duck's cab. Actually, it was a boom mike being extended from an NBC News van that had been assigned to cover the action. A reporter who looked a little like a younger William Holden complete with rolled-up sleeves and unbuttoned collar was hanging out of the van window and speaking through a bullhorn.

"Uh, Rubber Duck," he called.

"Yeah."

"Dave Raymond, NBC News."

Dave Raymond! Melissa looked up excitedly. She'd thought that voice sounded familiar. She leaned across the Duck to speak.

"Dave. Hi." she called. "Isn't this something?"

The reporter stared at her in disbelief. Being a newsman first, he passed the bullhorn to someone inside the van and shouted, "Cut!" before answering.

"Jesus, how'd you get here?" he called to Melissa, ignoring the Duck for the time being. "Who are you working for?"

"Nobody. It just happened," Melissa shouted back past the Duck's nose.

"You always were a great little kidder, Melissa. Come on. "I'll buy the pictures, notes. Top dollar."

Melissa shook her head. "Can't help you. Lost my cameras. And I don't care . . ."

Raymond ignored her. He gestured to one of the photographers in the van to take off his Nikon. Then he made a throwing motion toward Melissa, who hesitated. What must the Duck be thinking?

"Come on, take it," Raymond called. "Pay me back in film."

This time he did throw the camera, almost nailing the Duck on the chin with it. Melissa reached out instinctively to catch it as it flew by her. It was in her hands. It was hers.

"Where's Jack?" Raymond asked conversationally now that business had been arranged.

"We split. All over. I'm on my way to Brazil."

Raymond made a face. "Again? How many times does this make that you've 'split for good?' Aw, you'll be back together before you know it."

"But I don't want to be," Melissa protested.

"What they all say, kid. Listen I got to get back to this interview. We can't keep running in the opposite lane forever. Catch you later."

Since he had been situated smack in the middle of the conversation, the Duck couldn't help but take everything in, including the part about Bill. His glance toward Melissa was cool as she slid back to her seat, holding her new camera.

"Mr. Duck," Raymond was back on the bullhorn again. "Perhaps you could tell our news cameras what's going on out here. We have reports that you refused to stop at a roadblock and threatened to blow up your truck and kill all the police. Are you carrying explosives?"

"Yessir. That's right. Sure am."

"Then why are you refusing to stop? And also refusing to obey the speed limit."

"Because that's what convoys do," the Duck answered flatly. "They don't stop and they don't obey speed limits."

"But that's breaking the law on a big scale. What's the reason?"

The Duck began rolling up his window. Raymond gave it a last try. "Tell us what you're protesting about," he shouted.

At his words, Melissa jerked to attention. Of course. What a perfect, simple idea. She grabbed Duck's arm to prevent him closing the window any further.

"That's it," she cried excitedly. "You're protesting."

The Duck was thoroughly pissed off at both of them. "The hell I am," he growled.

"No, wait," Melissa continued. "Maybe it would work for

you. Tell them you're a protest march. Civil disobedience. It could get you off the hook?"

The Duck shook his head. "I got enough troubles . . ." he began.

But Melissa had not even started to give up. "Look, now you're just a common criminal. And you've committed felonies. So have all your friends back there. I think it's your only chance."

When the Duck still seemed reluctant to accept the truth of what she was saying, Melissa leaned over him and called out to Raymond.

"We're going to Washington, D.C., where we're going to file a class action suit against the United States government and seven of the major oil companies."

She pulled her head back into the cab and took the Duck's hand.

"Understand? I've worked in TV news. Trust me, I know about this stuff."

"I understand what you're doin, all right," the Duck answered stubbornly. "I just don't like it."

Melissa lost her temper then. "I get it," she snapped. "You want to go to jail. You like the security."

The indignation in her voice won him over as much as the logic of her argument. He gave her a sheepish smile.

"Aw, shit," he drawled, "you know, you ain't half smart."

"That's an understatement." The coals of Melissa's anger hadn't completely gone out.

The Duck unrolled the window and yelled over to Raymond, "Bring back your mike. I'll talk to you."

When the boom reappeared outside he didn't even wait for a question.

"Yeah. We're headin right up to Washington, D.C. The way I see it, it's the workingman against all that Government red tape and stupidity . . ."

Raymond sat back smiling in the van and let the recorders roll. This was the kind of interview he'd come out here for. The real stuff.

Just as the van pulled off at a side road and headed back to Albuquerque to process the completed interview for the evening news, a new voice came on the CB. It was a young voice, kittenish with more than a trace of cat in it.

"Hello. Calling everybody. Calling everybody. My name is Darlene and I'm five foot three. I have blue eyes and blonde hair, and I'm hitching east here at Marker 345. Is there any trucker out there who would really enjoy my company? Do you *read* me? *Come* on."

Suddenly for the first time since it formed, chaos broke out in the convoy. What had been a straight, orderly column became, in seconds, a mad scramble as trucks tried to pass each other on both shoulders of the highway, each determined to be the first to meet this siren of the road.

Since its triumphant passage through Allington, the convoy had slowed out of respect for some of its vehicles who weren't equipped to maintain a cross-country diesel pace. Now, the Duck slowed even more to give the boys room. Pig Pen was one of the first to come by, duelling fender to fender with a big White that was hauling a load of lumber. After a couple of indecisive bumps, the Love Machine shouldered the White off the road and into a barbed wire fence. The flying truck took out fifty yards of posts and fencing before it finally floundered to a stop, its load still miraculously intact. An even bigger Peterbilt took its place in the front line.

Darlene waved excitedly when she saw the trucks first appear around a curve about a mile away. A ride at last. But as they came closer, and she saw that there were *five* big rig diesels charging down the highway shoulder to shoulder, side by side, her joy turned to stark terror.

There was nowhere to run! She tried left, then right, and finally had to settle for the puny protection of a single telephone pole. She pressed herself up behind it, closed her eyes, and quivered. The deafening roar of the engines suddenly gave way to a truly tremendous cacophony of five sets of air brakes, uncountable times squealing, trailers banging and jackknifing off each other.

When Darlene opened her eyes again, there were five truckers standing in front of her, all trying to speak at once. In her present confused condition only bits and pieces came through: "I got a truck and roll." "Water bed with velvet trim." "Custom Award winner." "He's married. Darlin, I'll take you for the ride of your life."

She had never been so flattered in all her life. She blushed. Her eyelashes fluttered. When there was a lull in the presentations, she said, "Well, I'm just not sure."

Before they could get started again, she reached a decision. She would let Fate decide. She made them line up in front of her.

"Eenie, meenie, miny, moe . . ." she began. The final finger came to rest on Pig Pen. She stepped out of line and took her arm before the Fates had a chance to include any unforeseen postscripts.

"Bless you darlin," he said fervently. "Right this way."

He pointed out his rig and she smiled, happy that the gods had chosen such a beautiful big truck for her. She thought he was the one who kept talking about his waterbed. It was almost perfect. But as they approached closer, she got a simultaneous view and whiff of his load.

"My gosh," she murmured involuntarily.

Pig Pen knew he had to act fast before she changed her mind. He cupped his hand under her elbow and rushed her into the truck.

"Don't worry, darlin," he said quickly as he slammed the door behind him. "The stink blows back behind. All those others in back is the ones that got to worry."

"But . . ." she started a delicate, bewildered protest.

Pig Pen had already rushed around the cab and was climbing in the other door.

"You just sit back and relax," he reassured her. "Old Love Machine is gonna take you for a *ride*."

The Duck laughed to Melissa as they drove by Pig Pen and the other four disgruntled drivers. "That's old Pig Pen," he chuckled. "Lookit that. Four other truckers and he scores easy as pie."

"Breaker, Breaker," the Widow Woman's voice came over the CB. "How come you ain't in that, Spider Mike. You're young and frisky."

"You know I'm savin myself for you, Widow Woman," Spider Mike came back.

The Duck picked up the microphone. "You watch yourself, Mike," he kidded. "She'll do you in, the way she did the last four of her husbands."

"Aw, go sit on a cold carrot, Duck," the Widow Woman snapped back. "Every one of my husbands died happy men. I done loved them to death."

Melissa was smiling at the CB chatter and sipping on a beer from the cooler at the back corner of Duck's sleeper. "You know what," she said, feeling good, "I have to get myself a handle."

The Duck wasn't through bullshitting. "How about Bucket Mouth," he suggested sweetly.

"Come on. I'm serious."

"I got it. There you go." The Duck was pointing at a road sign that read, DANGEROUS CURVES.

"Dangerous curves?" Melissa looked down at her body. It was nice, she liked it a lot. It was lean and trim and round where it should be round, but it wasn't a body to stop traffic on the street or the beach. She shook her head. "No. I don't think that's me."

The Duck gave her a good looking over. She began to feel uncomfortable as his eyes traveled over her, stopping just long enough at all the right spots.

"I don't know about that," he answered judiciously.

"Well, thank you, but let's get another." Melissa was having more trouble than usual with her poise. She told herself it was because of this whole crazy trip, The Duck was grinning at her.

"Got it," he announced triumphantly. "Mother Trucker."

"Beautiful. Just beautiful." She sat back and folded her arms in resignation. "Dangerous Curves it is."

The Duck reached over and gave her a friendly slug on the arm. "Cheer up," he said, "It could be worse."

"Yeah," she answered, punching him back with maybe a little more affection than she thought she intended, "it could be Rubber Duck."

Meanwhile a little further down the line, Pig Pen was just charming the be-Jesus out of his passenger.

"See, didn't I tell you," he crowed. "Can't smell a thing, can you?"

Darlene sniffed the air delicately. "No," she admitted as if she still didn't quite believe it.

"Yup, the wind leaves the smell behind," Pig Pen allowed with a degree of satisfaction. "Har, har. Want to see my sleeper."

Without waiting for an answer, he reached back and unzipped the leather partition behind the seat. Darlene gave the infamous whorehouse sleeper the once-over. It didn't seem to faze her any. Jesus, Pig Pen thought, half in fright and half in glee, maybe she's one of those really innocent ones.

"That's a waterbed," he explained thoughtfully, almost assuming the role of a tour guide in his effort to be very cool. "And real velvet there. And you like music? I got quad."

She shuffled through his pile of eight tracks and finally shoved one into the player. It turned out to be the music from "Last Tango in Paris", possibly Pig Pen's all-time favorite movie. He looked over at her. There she sat – slim, young, stacked, and by God right there in his cab. He couldn't believe it, simply couldn't believe it.

"You'll like ridin' with me," he said suddenly, giving her his most suggestive grin for good measure. Darlene lowered her eyes shyly. He could see that he'd have to soften her up a little. God damn, this was almost fun. He assumed the mantle of world-weariness, the wise old man of the Road.

"I don't know," he began without bothering to specify what, "these long lonely days on the road can really get you down. Like the song says, it's sad to be alone. Still, I got my work to think about. I gotta get these go-go girls back there into Washington, D.C., by tomorrow. Government property. But maybe I shouldn't be telling you that?"

"Telling me what?" So far Darlene was not overly into his story.

"About the government. I'm not at liberty to talk about it."

"Why? Is it some kind of secret?"

Pig Pen could sense a slight rise in her curiosity level and poured it on.

"Well, let's put it this way. Don't it seem a little odd that a rig like this, I mean with your pink rabbit fur side panelling and all, would be carrying just any old stinking hogs. Don't that seem a little strange?"

"Now that you mention it . . ." Darlene was getting sucked in despite herself.

Pig Pen leaned closer, prepared to share a humungous secret. "These are not your ordinary pigs," he confided, carefully keeping his voice level with just an edge of tension. "These are *government* pigs."

Darlene was either impressed because she was confused, or confused because she was impressed, or both of the above at once.

"They have something to do with the swine flu maybe?" she ventured timidly.

Pig Pen gave her a wise wink.

"Possibly. Possibly something to do with behind the Iron Curtain. But maybe I've said too much already. Why don't we talk about you."

"Me? There's nothing very exciting in my life."

"Well, that's a good idea hitchin with the CB like that." Pig Pen labored to keep the conversation afloat. "Where you headed?"

"East."

One syllable answers weren't going to make it, Pig Pen knew too well. He'd have to keep her talking.

"You look sorta like Giselle McKenzie, anybody ever tell you that?" he said suddenly, apropos of absolutely nothing except his need to keep the conversation going somehow.

"No." Darlene cast an appraising eye around the cab. "You know, this really is a very nice truck you've got here."

Pig Pen kicked back and concentrated on the road. This was his favorite subject. He could talk about it in his sleep, and sometimes did.

"Yeah, I put a lot of work into it. Over two thousand dollars worth of chrome alone. Plus all the little luxury items inside. You seen the mirrors in the sleeper? You know, I coulda got just plain stereo, but quad is . . ."

While Pig Pen had been extolling the virtues of the Love Machine, Darlene had been busily undressing and revealing virtues of a somewhat different kind.

She had stripped down to her bra and panties before Pig

Pen noticed. His voice trailed off. He stared at her in utter stupification "Damn," he muttered to himself. "I knew women liked my truck, but . . ."

A sudden hardness came across Darlene's face, the pitiless cruelty of the kill. Even her voice had changed, become deadly.

"I'm under eighteen years old and I'm going to scream rape," she said.

Pig Pen's mind was totally blown. All he could manage was a "What?"

Suddenly she began a high-pitched, elongated scream that pierced his head like a knife. "R a a a a p e."

"Wait. Stop!" he begged. "Somebody will . . ."

She stopped.

"What's wrong with you?" he demanded in the silence that still seemed to be ringing in his ears. "I never touched you."

"I know you didn't," she replied calmly, "but I'm screaming rape, and I'm getting on the radio and screaming rape." She paused and tore one side of her panties to emphasize her point. "And I ain't going to stop unless you give me twenty-five dollars."

"I got a ticket back in Arizona where this whole thing started. I ain't got twenty-five dollars."

Darlene was not one for long arguments. "Rape! Rape! Rape!" she screamed. She reached for the CB, but Pig Pen stopped her.

"Okay, okay," he surrendered. "Just shut up that screamin. It goes right through my head."

He reached into a secret compartment built into the sun-visor and took out a bill.

"Do you have any change?" he asked hopefully. "I've only got a hundred."

Darlene gasped. It was a C-note for sure. She grabbed the bill from his hand. "That'll do," she said, tucking it down the front of her panties, the safest place she could think of, dressed as she was.

"Now wait a minute," Pig Pen protested.

"I'll scream," Darlene warned. "those other truckers will tear you apart."

Pig Pen shut up.

"Now pull over and let me out at the next intersection," she continued more calmly. One was coming up in the distance. She began to slip back into her clothes. As they approached the crossroads. Pig Pen slowed and began to pull over.

"By the way," she said, her hand on the door release, "if you're gettin any ideas about after I get out, don't. I can call rape on you any time I want. I got witnesses."

Pig Pen applied the brakes and brought the Love Machine to a stop. While it was still rolling the final few feet, Darlene jumped out and slammed the door behind her.

"Bye, bye, chump," she called through the half open window.

"Don't you ever tell nobody you did this to me," Pig Pen blustered. "Don't tell nobody, hear! Nobody. I'll murder you."

On his way by, Nasty Mike blasted a salute on his air horn. Pig Pen turned and flipped him the bird. "Aw shut up," he growled mostly to himself. He gave Darlene, who had modestly turned her back, a final look that was a masterful mixture of rage and bone-weary sadness. He revved up the engine and worked his way back in line.

Most but not all of the convoy had passed by the time Darlene was able to maneuver Pig Pen's hundred into what she considered a safer spot. She stepped back to the curb, a smile on her face, thumb out. She had the feeling that this was going to be her lucky day.

About forty miles south in Vaughn, the TV in the Flying Eagle Truck Stop Bar and Grill, was carrying the Duck's interview on the NBC Weekend News.

A lone trucker, Bubba, and Madge, the fortyish swing shift waitress, were idly watching the show when the Duck suddenly appeared on the screen, driving his truck and talking a mile a minute.

"Yeah. We're headin right up to Washington. It's the workingman against all that government red tape and overregulation."

"And what about the oil prices?" Melissa prompted. Throughout the interview she could be seen in the background snapping shots of Duck with her Nikon while he talked.

"Yeah, on top of that, how about these oil prices?" he continued, his voice growing angrier and more determined by the minute. "Big oil companies, they're makin double, three times what they used to make, and they're tellin the rest of us to take it in the shorts."

Bubba suddenly let out a cheer. "Talk that talk, man," he called out to the image on the screen. "Get *down* there with them bastards."

"You don't see them politicians tellin the oil companies to take it for a change," the Duck's image said, doing just that. Nossir. And they lyin to us . . . don't tell anybody how much they got and where they got it. Well, maybe we're gonna find out. If them politicians won't put the screws on, we will."

"Damn," Bubba exploded. "That's me."

"What?" Madge had been thinking that that driver on the tube was a pretty good looking stud.

"I got to be part of that." Bubba stood up and headed for the door.

"You leavin?" Madge said, surprised. "You don't have a load to haul."

"Then I'll take the tractor, but by God I'm goin."

Men are crazy, Madge reflected. The program had moved on to a commercial about owning a piece of the rock.

But all over western New Mexico the word was out. In a half dozen truck stops clear to the Texas border diesels were fired up and headed out to become part of the convoy. A group of Satan's Mother's cut short their picnic and fired up their irons. Nobody needed to tell them where the action was. In the little town of Casper's Corners, Eighteenwheel Eddie, who boasted over four years for every wheel in his handle, was making it down the street in his three-wheel invalid cart, all the while talking excitedly in the CB.

"Break one-nine for Eighteenwheel Eddie. I'm screwin it down in my cabover Pete heading for rendezvous at marker 415. And I say damn the double nickel."

Back in the convoy itself, Melissa was hanging out the Duck's window trying for some panoramic shots against the backdrop of the late afternoon sun. She pulled herself back inside and began changing the film.

"Pretty soon I'm going to need a telescopic lens just to keep everybody in sight," she complained happily.

They laughed. "Before we're through, we'll have a convoy stretchin clear across the whole damn state."

Which was precisely the problem that Governor Haskins and his two top aides were in the process of thrashing out in the conference room of the Governor's mansion in Santa Fé. In his late thirties, Haskins was one of the new breed of politicians, young, shrewd, uncommitted to any party line or platform. He had been elected to his present term by the narrowest of margins, and there was another election looming in the not too distant horizon.

The two men with him seemed to have been chosen to contrast with each other, which was in fact the case. Concerned primarily with which image would most benefit him, Haskins liked to hear both extremes on Crucial issues before making a decision. Later on, when the chips were down, the stakes higher on the national level, he could afford to take a stand.

The older of the two aides, Henry (Big Hank) Meyers, had been a force in state politics longer than Haskins had been eligible to vote. A veteran of back rooms and hundred dollar a plate fundraisers, he was the voice of experience in the group. The other man, Chuck Arnoldi, was not yet half big Hank's age. A former third string All-American fullback at the University of New Mexico, he was starting up the ladder from gridiron to at least the Statehouse someday. All three men were watching a TV, which for the past hour had been given over to presenting coverage and commentary on the convoy's progress.

"Absolutely, absolutely yes." Meyers gave the conference table a couple of emphatic thumps. "You've got a real old-time showdown here."

"I agree. It's great stuff for the campaign," Arnoldi put in, his eyes fixed to the tube. The screen was suddenly filled with a crowd of bystanders cheering the convoy.

"Did you see that lady trucker?" the Governor asked amused. "She gave the police the finger."

"I tell you, you couldn't ask for a better chance to make the headlines. The National Guard is already on alert. Mobilize."

"Sure, and think about Kent State, too," Arnoldi challenged. "All we need is a scene like that and goodbye election."

"You should watch this, Henry," Haskins said thoughtfully to the older man. "It's a hell of a thing."

Meyers snorted. "Truckers and bikers, Riffraff."

The Governor shook his head. "Not the crowds we've been seeing in the last half-hour. They're average people – voters. Did you notice those 'Welcome Convoy' banners they've been putting up? To tell you the truth, I'm beginning to think this convoy has more public support than we do."

For a moment, they watched the television in silence. There was a rerun of the convoy running a red light, then a closeup of a matron in a shopping center talking a mile a minute on the CB in her station wagon.

"But why are they doing all this?" Meyers broke out in exasperation. "It can't be just the speed limit, can it?"

"That and I suppose they find the anarchy of the thing attractive," Haskins answered calmly.

"Well, isn't that the point? They're breaking the *law*, and it's important for you to make a reputation as a law and order man."

"Let's not get carried away, Henry. Your chauffeur breaks the law every day. Want me to call out the Guard on you?"

For the moment, Meyers was silenced. The man had a point. But still . . .

The Governor turned to Arnoldi. "Chuck, I hope you're ready for a little trip. You've got an invitation to deliver."

The young aide leaped to his feet. This was the way he'd hoped it would go, with a nice bit of public exposure for him in the bargain.

"What are you suggesting?" Meyers demanded, half-afraid that he already knew.

The Governor turned his attention back to the TV. A group of girl scouts were shown strewing flowers over the hood of the Duck's cab.

"If you can't kill em," he said quietly, "kiss em."

Back in the convoy, Melissa was almost beside herself with exhilaration. Everything was going better than she could possibly have dreamed. The public support was enormous, and building with every town they passed through. Outside it was growing dark, the twilight being hurried along by a bank of storm clouds racing down from the north. She became aware of a sudden ticking, scratching noise that enveloped the truck from front to rear. The Duck said, "Damn," softly and began to pull over on the shoulder of the road.

"What is it?" she asked in alarm. "What's wrong?"

Ignoring her, he reached for the CB.

"Looks like we got us a real ditch digger," he announced. "Best shut em down and cover up."

"What's going on?" she demanded. "Why are we stopping here?"

The Duck set the emergency brake and pointed out the windshield. The visibility had gone to zero.

"Sandstorm," he answered bluntly. He turned off the engine and began to stretch some of the kink out of his back and shoulders. "Ain't nothin we can do, but wait her out and see what happens next."

CHAPTER SIX

THE sudden storm caught everybody by surprise. For Lyle, it was another in what was becoming a continuing series of disasters. His plan had been a simple one, virtually foolproof. The roadblock fiasco had shown him that, whatever those two FBI turds might think, nothing short of the U.S. Army was likely to put a stop to that damn convoy. It had become a gigantic missile with that Rubber Jerk's truck as a very touchy warhead. Damn – as thoroughly pissed off as he was, Lyle had to admire the way the man went at the roadblock.

But if you couldn't stop them direct, there were other ways. As the son and grandson of ranchers, Lyle had seen how the wolfpacks used to hang on to the edges of the main herd at the roundup time. There were always stragglers, those who couldn't keep up the pace, or just wandered off by themselves from time to time. He'd known the wolves to follow a herd for miles, sometimes days, just waiting for their chance. Eventually, one of the steers would come up lame or stray a little too far, and then the pack became unbelievably quick, sure and deadly.

And that was exactly what Lyle aimed to be. Also, in the back of his mind was the possibility that the whole convoy might spook if he picked off a few of them. If they did stampede, he had his number one, two and three targets all picked out. The excitement of that thought brought on his favorite fantasy – his name in the national headlines, speeches, maybe even a parade. He could see it now:

CONVOY HALTED

LYLE WALLACE CORRALS LEADERS

That was the plan. He had pulled a few strings, got himself deputized, and requisitioned an unmarked car from the

Allington Police Department. That had taken a little time, but he wasn't worried. By then, all he had to do was watch TV or listen to the radio to find out just exactly where those sons of bitches were and what they were doing.

Catching up proved to be a little more difficult. Although it had slowed some since Allington, the convoy was still screwin it down pretty good and they didn't stop for hell nor high water along the way neither. At first Lyle was tempted to put on the siren and lights and just rip through those little towns the way they did. But with all those TV people coming and going, it wasn't safe. If he called attention to himself, he might as well quit before he started.

So he took all the short cuts and bypasses he could find on the map, including a couple that deadended in farmyards, and kept his speed at a hundred or better outside the populated areas, which luckily for him were few and far between in this part of the state. He had been almost within striking distance when this goddamn storm came up out of nowhere and did some striking of its own.

He refused to believe it, which was his first mistake. He reduced his speed and plowed on, his second and nearly fatal miscalculation. A sudden gust of gale force wind threw a blinding curtain of sand across his windshield and literally blew him off the road. He slowed to a stop, hubcap deep in the loose sand that lined the road beyond the shoulder. He gunned the motor, trying to pop the tires loose and ended up buried even worse.

He climbed out of the downwind door with the vague idea of sliding something under the wheels and almost got his head blown off. After a moment of sheer panic, he crawled back in, half blind and spitting sand like a beached whale. He didn't guess he'd ever get all of it out of his nose and ears.

He ground his teeth in pure rage, which served mostly to remind him that he hadn't yet cleared all of the grit from his mouth either, and reached for the radio. After a couple of false starts and a lot of cross traffic from what seemed to be at least fifty ten-year old kids all talking about the storm on their CBs, he managed to reach the garage he'd passed ten miles back at a crossroads, only to discover that the owner-operator-mechanic-and-tow-truck driver had gone to his niece's home for a family reunion and wouldn't be back until late. He couldn't be reached by phone because the lines were down. When the storm was over, somebody could drive out and get him. It was only forty miles, and if Lyle kept on using that kind of language, maybe they wouldn't go at all.

He snapped off the radio and started to sulk. After about five minutes of that and nothing else, he began to bore himself and came out of it. After all, in this weather, the convoy wasn't going anywhere either. He discovered a last month's *Hustler* folded over and stuffed beneath the front seat. Things weren't so bad. At least he had something to read.

Hamilton and Fish weren't particularly happy themselves. After the Allington debacle, they had taken the chopper to the National Guard Armory in Santa Fé where they planned to help coordinate the anticipated mobilization. The Governor's decision had caught them, and the Guard, completely by surprise.

The Guard remained on alert. Hamilton and Fish remained stranded – seventy-five miles from the action with no way of getting back to it. Thinking that they would be traveling with the Guard, they had dispatched their copter back to Albuquerque shortly after their arrival at the Armory. When they were informed of the Governor's plan to confer with, rather than demolish, the convoy, they headed immediately for the State Commander's office.

The Commander, a General Ralston, who looked a little like a character out of the *Beetle Bailey* comic strip, had been seated at his desk with his head in his hands. When he heard them come in, he raised it slightly and said, "You've heard the Governor's decision, gentlemen?"

Struck by the real anguish in his voice, they looked at each other, then nodded.

The General removed his head from his hands long enough to shake it dolefully several times. "A terrible thing, gentlemen," he said. It was obvious that he was still in shock. "A terrible thing."

"From our experience with this convoy, I wouldn't predict much success in talking with them," Fish put in tactfully.

The General shook his head a couple more times, then stood up and walked to the window. Outside, since the storm had passed east of Santa Fé, a beautifully tranquil sunset complete with fleecy orange clouds was settling softly over the town. Suddenly, he pulled himself erect and turned back to the two agents.

"I say blow them to hell," he thundered. "They've been warned."

"Well, General, let's hope that doesn't become necessary," Hamilton replied diplomatically.

The older man glared at him.

"Let's hope it does."

After the silence that the remark seemed to demand, Hamilton tried again. As a recruit, he had been given training in how to get along with people, but between that Arizona cop and now this fruitcake, this was turning into the weirdest case of his career.

"What we've really come for, General," he began as placatingly as possible, "is transportation. We need to requisition a copter to get back to the action."

The General gave no sign of having heard him. His fighting blood was up, his mind on battles no one else would ever know. When he looked up his eyes were fierce.

"Not a chance, gentlemen. We are on Alert."

"But surely . . ." Fish interrupted.

"It is imperative that all personnel and equipment be maintained in battle-ready condition," the General continued, ignoring him.

"But General, this is just a convoy, not a war," Hamilton objected.

The General fixed them both with a steely glare. Wiseass Federal whippersnappers.

"Not yet," he answered ominously. "In any case, I have my orders, gentlemen, and I intend to carry them out. Good day."

"Jesus," Fish said when they were outside the door. "If this is our side, maybe we ought to join the convoy."

"Don't think I haven't considered it," Hamilton answered wrily. "The way we're going, they'll end up controlling at least a couple of states by default."

Driving back to the action was out of the question since the storm had moved in directly across their route to the convoy. They headed for the radio room.

"Call operations in Albuquerque and tell them to send the chopper back as soon as it gets there," Hamilton ordered the operator on duty. He took a quarter from his pocket and placed it on his thumb.

"Call it in the air," he said to Fish. "Let's see who pays for the coffee this time."

Governor Haskins was pissed. That Goddamned storm was screwing him up royally. His plan had called for a lightning stroke. Arnoldi was to fly to Tucumcari, arrange for the use of the Municipal Park for the meeting, and then drive west to meet the convoy and present the Governor's proposal. Everything was to have been concluded almost before it could be announced.

The first part had gone smoothly enough. The park was available and already being cleared for the convoy's arrival. But then that idiot Arnoldi had driven straight into the storm and disappeared as completely as if he'd dropped down a hole. Even radio communication had been disrupted for the past half hour.

As the time lagged between the official announcement of the Governor's proposal and any word of its acceptance by the convoy, the pressure had begun to mount. That old fool over at the National Guard had been on the phone every ten minutes with his 'blood and iron' complaints. The Civil Liberties Union had publically endorsed the Governor's stand, but the police chiefs of two of the towns that had been overrun by the convoy had issued statements denouncing him as a milksop. As usual, the League of Women Voters didn't know which way to go. Elections had been won and lost on less. "Jesus Christ, Arnoldi," he muttered to himself, shaking his clenched fist at God or whatever might lie above, "Where in hell are you?"

Where Arnoldi was, was the Dry Hole Saloon, a tiny weatherbeaten shack on a crossroads, just east of Tucumcari, and he was having quite a time. Luckily he had been passing by just as the storm forced him to pull over. Once inside, he had let it slip casually that he was an aide to Governor Haskins on a special mission to the convoy. After all, these people were voters, and a little positive public exposure never hurt. Then he let it get out somehow that he'd played a little football down the road at the University, and the bartender insisted on buying him another beer. When he was about halfway through it, a grizzled old man who looked as though he'd grown out of the desert like the yuccas and Joshua trees, stumped up the length of the bar and confronted him.

"You're the Governor's man," he stated, not really making it a question.

Arnoldi nodded. "You bet I am."

"Tell me, what kind of deal you gonna make those fellers out there in them trucks?"

"I'm afraid I'm not at liberty to disclose that information at this time." It was a line Arnoldi used practically every day in the press conferences at the Capital. The man took his time getting the words straight.

"Well, I'll tell you this," he said finally, "if you don't give them truckers a fair shake, you're gonna have us and a whole lot like us to deal with. Ain't that right, boys?"

The other six or so inhabitants of the bar made their agreement known with assorted grunts and curses.

"I assure you that the Governor's proposal is more than fair," Arnoldi stammered. He was beginning to feel like a decided minority.

The old man snorted to show what he thought of politicians and their proposals. He fixed Arnoldi with an angry stare.

"It better be," he growled accusingly, and clumped back to his stool.

Shaken, Arnoldi turned back to his beer. He found that he was drinking alone.

When the sand began flying, the convoy hadn't needed the Duck's orders to pull to a halt. One after another, like planes in those World War II movies, they peeled out of formation and hit the shoulder of the highway. The four Satans Mothers who remained in the convoy were put in the box of a furniture hauler who was running empty, where they immediately lit up and began to get down.

"Hey, Pig Pen," Spider Mike called. "Ain't this a bitch?"

"Sure looks like one. Course it's as bad on the bears as it is on us," Pig Pen came on.

"What about them go-go girls of yourn? Think they'll be all right?"

"Number one, they ain't my go-go girls. I'm just haulin em. Number two, did you ever try to kill one of them critters? They're survivors, man. I can tell you that for damn certain. I figure that sand out there might do em some good, clean em up a little."

"Amen to that, old buddy. They's startin to make my eyes water back here. What we gonna do now?"

This was no idle question. Most of the long haulers in the convoy were already pretty jacked up with amphetamines, and being cooped up in a cab by a sandstorm, especially with all the problems they had nibbling at the edges of their minds, was no light matter. Paranoia was only a split second away.

"If you ain't got nothin better, I can read you some from this here novel," the Widow Woman offered.

"What's it called?" Big Nasty wanted to know.

"*Heathcliffe House.*"

"What's it about?" somebody back near the end of the convoy asked dubiously.

"If you'll shut your yap," Pig Pen broke in peevishly, "we'll all find out. Go ahead, Widow Woman."

She cleared her throat and began to read in a stiff monotone: " 'Agatha sat gazing long into her boudoir mirror, dreaming of him, his strong arms, his manly loins. Would the day ever come when Errol would make her his?' "

"Jesus Christ," Big Nasty exploded. Somebody further down the line made a sound like puking.

"Well, if you don't like it," the Widow Woman said in a hurt voice, "I'll just read to myself."

"Hey, you guys," a new voice entered into the conversation, "shut your holes. It's better than nothin."

"So's gettin your ass kicked," Big Nasty growled, "but not a hell of a lot."

"So turn off your squawker and shut up so's the rest of us can hear," Spider Mike suggested.

"With pleasure. I wouldn't wipe my ass on that crap."

"Go ahead, Widow Woman," Pig Pen coaxed after an interval of silence. "Don't pay any attention to shit-for-brains back there. I liked that part about the manly loins. Whenever they start in like that, it means there's somethin pretty good comin up soon."

" 'Behind her, the drapes swayed softly as if from the faintest breeze, but it was a windless night. Could it be? "Errol?" she called breathlessly, her hand on her breast to still her wildly beating heart. The curtain parted to reveal not the graceful form of her lover, but the brutish figure of Jason Wilkins, the overseer, his eyes on fire with lust.' "

"See?" Pig Pen crowed. "What did I tell ya? Right on, Widow Woman. Hammer Down!"

For a long time after he had turned off the engine the Duck sat silently staring at the sand spattered windshield. His eyes were tense, vacant with thought. Melissa began to fidget. Taking no notice, he continued whatever internal debate or analysis had captured him. Finally, when the tension had become close to unbearable, she took a penny from her pocket and tossed it on his lap.

"For your thoughts," she answered to his questioning glance. "If you're going to think it, you might as well say it."

"It appears to me that I been doin just a shitload more talkin than I ought, already."

"What do you mean?"

He sat back with a sigh and lit a cigarette before answering.

"It's like this, the way I figure it. I been shootin off my mouth to them reporters all day 'bout what *we* want and what this convoy's all about."

"So?"

"So what if I don't know what I'm talkin about?"

"Do you?"

"Maybe I do, maybe I don't," he answered slowly. "But one thing's for damn sure. I ain't no spokesman for anybody."

"If you aren't, who is? The politicians? the oil companies? maybe the police?"

He shook his head as if he was trying to jiggle a bunch of pieces into place. "I don't know," he answered. "I was reflectin on that when somebody stuck her nose in a while ago."

"I'm sorry. Do you want to go back to it?"

"Naw. Shit I wasn't gettin nowhere, anyhow. I'm thinkin that maybe it's one of those things you never do study out. You just jump on and ride to the end of the line, and that's what it was. Let's talk about somethin else."

"Okay, where are you from?"

The Duck smiled at the trace of a professional interviewer's tone that had crept into her voice. He looked around the cab.

"You're sittin in it," he said. "I was born in El Paso, and I currently got a place in Albuquerque to hang my clothes. What about you?"

She patted the two suitcases stashed in the sleeper. "That's it. I gave up the place I used to hang them in L.A. two days ago."

"Where you headed?"

She spread her hands, palms up.

"What about the guy that reporter was talkin about?"

"Jack? That's over. It was all just a big mistake."

"From what I heard, it appears to be the kind of mistake you made a couple more times than once."

"So what? What's it to you?" He had pushed the wrong button. Her mind began filling with further things she wanted to say, angry things.

"I'm sorry," he said, with a sincerity that short-circuited her rage. "I guess I'm gettin a little spooked by this whole damn situation. I never wanted it."

He paused, and when she didn't say anything, continued talking in a quieter, almost hesitant voice.

"I was thinkin that now everything's changed so we don't rightly even know who's chasin who anymore . . . Well, I was thinkin that if you want out, I suppose I could drop you just about anywhere."

"Are you kidding?" Melissa patted the Nikon on the seat between them. "The biggest break of my career was when I stowed away in that sleeper. These pictures are worth thousands, more than that if I decided to do a book later on. And besides . . ."

"And what?" the Duck's voice was flooded with a cold rage. Generations of being exploited poured out in the two words. Melissa recoiled from the intensity of his reaction.

She was neither a coward or a fool. "And besides, I was going to say, this has become a lot more than an assignment. There's something real going on here, something important. I don't know what it is. I don't think any of you know yet either. But pictures or no pictures, I want to be part of it."

"Sure." The Duck had heard this kind of thing before.

"Well, what do you want me to do?" she cried in exasperation. "Throw away the film? What the hell good would that do?"

He gave her a level look that went right through her.

"That depends on how much of a part of all this you really want to be," he said evenly.

The voice of the Widow Woman penetrated the silence between them. " 'Oh Errol, Errol. I'll always love you.' "

Holding the Duck's eyes with her own, Melissa reached out and picked the Nikon off the seat. She sprung open the loading hatch and removed the half-exposed roll of film. She unzipped the side pocket of her purse and took out the roll of film she'd shot that afternoon. With a mocking smile, she held out the two rolls for him to see. Then she rolled down her window and tossed them out into the storm.

"Well?" she challenged.

The Duck looked at her closely, as if for the first time. By God, here was a real woman. It had been so long since he'd come across one that he'd forgotten they were still around.

" 'Oh, Errol. We mustn't,' " the Widow Woman put in.

"You ever been married?" he asked suddenly.

"Once. It didn't work out."

"Well, to my way of thinkin, whoever the man was, he surely missed his chance."

" 'Errol, Errol.' " the Widow Woman cooed, really into her reading at last.

"Notice anything?"

Melissa's mind was a blur of thoughts, feelings, memories. She shook her head numbly.

"Listen." He turned down the radio.

It took her a half minute of intense effort to realize that there was no sound at all. The storm had passed.

The Duck clicked on the headlights. The highway ahead was clear. He took over the CB.

"This is the Duck, and in case you ain't noticed, it's boogie time. You all hang close, hear. No tellin what's ahead."

In almost perfect sequence, the line of trucks came alive like a pack of bright-eyed nocturnal animals. The Duck gave a blast on his air horn and pulled out onto the road. The convoy was on the move again.

For Lyle it wasn't quite so simple. When the storm let up, he tried to rock the car loose, got pissed off when that didn't work and gunned it just to show the goddamn thing who was boss. He succeeded in burying the back tires up to the fenders.

He finally roused the service station by threatening to personally get their CB license revoked if they refused to answer another damn time, only to find out that the owner, a Mr. Twitchell, had decided to stay the night at his niece's home.

"Tell you what," Lyle suggested as calmly as he could, "Why don't you shut down the pumps and bring that truck out here yourself? It's worth twenty bucks."

"Can't do that. Mr. Twitchell's drivin it."

Lyle didn't even bother to curse. He flagged down the first set of headlights coming his way, which turned out to be an old Ford pickup with two twenty to twenty-fiveish men in the cab. Between them on the seat was a half empty bottle of bourbon, which under the circumstances, Lyle thought it best to overlook.

"How about a tow?" he asked, indicating the silhouette of his car at the edge of their headlights.

The driver, who was prematurely balding and compensating with a full, scraggly beard, turned to his friend.

"What do you think, Tom? We got the time?"

Tom was a smaller man with a mustache that drooped over both corners of his mouth. His hair, which reached almost to his shoulders, was probably blond when it had been washed. He took a while to consider the situation.

"Don't know, Len," he finally allowed. "Them gals ain't

gonna stay warm forever." He turned to Lyle. "Course if it was to be worth our while . . ." he suggested.

"Just how much do you figure your while is worth?" Lyle wasn't about to haggle. He was already planning to badge them once the car was safely out on the highway. With that open bottle, they were sitting ducks.

Len calculated for a while. "Oh, I'd say in the neighborhood of twenty-five bucks," he said just as Lyle was about to begin making offers in order to get the negotiations under way. "Apiece," he added almost as an afterthought.

"Fifty bucks. That's a mite steep, ain't it?" Since he planned on getting it back anyway, Lyle would have agreed to a hundred and fifty but he didn't want them getting suspicious until he was out of that damn ditch.

Tom took a long, pointed look in both directions on the deserted highway.

"Depends on what your choice might be."

"Okay, you got me there," Lyle gave in. "Back her over here. I got some important business down the road."

Neither man moved.

"Now what?" Lyle demanded.

Len put out a hand, palm up. After a moment of awkward silence, Lyle counted the fifty dollars into it. When they had positioned the truck in front of Lyle's car, the two men got out and watched while Lyle pulled the cable out of the back and attached it to both bumpers. Then with almost ridiculous ease, they pulled the car out to the pavement and got out to watch Lyle unhook the cable. Now was his chance.

"I guess you fellas don't know who I am," he began.

"Guess not," Len agreed.

Lyle yanked out his wallet and flashed his badge. "Police officer."

"So?"

Len didn't seem particularly surprised. His friend was back fooling around with the tailgate and seemed to be out of the conversation.

"Well, it appeared to me when you drove up that you boys was doin some substantial drinkin. Open bottle in the cab. Could lose your license over that. Not to mention the fine. So the way I see it, your rates just went down. To nothin."

Len still didn't seem to be getting the point. He looked at Lyle with almost no change in expression.

"Could I see that badge again?" he asked.

Lyle handed him the billfold. Len held it in front of the headlights and studied the badge for a moment. Then he leafed through the bill compartment, which was stuffed with the money that Lyle had collected in fines that morning. Lyle held out his hand, but the other man made no move to return the wallet.

"That's an Arizona shield," he observed.

"Course it is. I'm on special assignment. Got deputized back in Allington this afternoon. This wasn't going exactly, or even at all the way Lyle had planned. Just then he felt a pinprick in his side. Only it wasn't no damn pin. The blade of Tom's knife had to be at least six inches long.

"You know," Len said offhandedly, counting the money in the wallet more purposefully, "if there's one thing we can't stand, absolutely can't, it's a cop. But there's one other thing worser'n that. And that's an out of state cop. We got more than enough of you pig fuckers right here at home."

As if in sympathy with those thoughts, Tom increased the pressure on the knife. Lyle was becoming definitely uncomfortable.

"You kill a cop and they'll fry your ass," he warned.

Len laughed. "We got no plans to dust you. Not less'n we should see you, or your pig buddies, again. But our rates just went back up." He removed the badge before he deposited the wallet in his pocket. "Here's your shield," he said. "You might need it when you get back home to Arizona."

"Now just a minute, you son of a bitch." For a moment Lyle forgot where he was. Those bastards had about fifteen bucks of his own money, plus the hundred and eighty he'd gotten off the Duck and his buddies that morning. It wasn't fair.

This time the knife broke the skin between his ribs with an almost audible pop like that of a tooth being pulled.

"Let me stick him, Len," Tom begged from behind Lyle's left shoulder. "There ain't nobody around."

"Naw," Len decided. "Too much hassle. Besides, you stick that nice shiny blade in shit like that, you're gonna ruin it."

He walked over to Lyle's car and ripped the CB antenna off the trunk. Then he tore out the wires and mike inside for good measure.

"Don't bother thankin us," he said. "It's our pleasure."

When the truck had disappeared back the way it had come, Lyle took a minute to catch his breath. He'd settle with those sons of bitches later, on his way back. He had their license number in his head and he wasn't ever likely to forget it. He started the car in motion toward the east and goosed it up to eight-five. Old Lyle was back on the trail. Those gearjammin bastards up ahead had just better watch their ass.

CHAPTER SEVEN

About seventy miles further down the road, those gear-jammin bastards were having quite a time. When the convoy hit the road after the storm, it was national news and produced an outburst of extraordinary reactions across the country.

In Kankeekee, Illinois, for example, crowds of people gathered in the street in front of a local TV store to cheer the convoy on and to follow its progress on a giant TV screen shrewdly set up in the show window by the proprietor. In several widely scattered locations across the States, collections were started to help defray the anticipated legal costs of the truckers, and a national coordinating committee began to form.

In Roanoke, Virginia, a Sunday evening prayer group added the convoy to the list of shut-ins and dearly departeds for which they begged particular divine favor. A rumor swept Miami Beach that the convoy was actually headed for Florida where a fleet of Cuban ships were gathered off the coast to carry the drivers to sanctuary.

A prominent civil rights attorney from Chicago offered over national television to take on the case of the Duck, Pig Pen and Spider Mike for a fraction of his usual fee. The FBI checked into the Duck's file, discovered no incriminating evidence, and ordered an intensive field investigation. Simultaneously a request was sent to the Pentagon for his service records, especially those covering his two years as a pilot in Vietnam.

The Capitol was buzzing – with the news of the convoy and otherwise. The senior senator from Alabama called for a committee investigation of the trucking industry. This was countered by a proposal from the Liberal Caucus to institute a full scale probe of the major oil companies, with particular emphasis on the impact of the fifty-five mile per hour speed limit on diesel fuel consumption in interstate commerce.

Convoy Parties sprang up in New York, Chicago, Denver and San Francisco. They took the absurd but appropriate form of thronging into busy intersections, hugging, kissing, blowing grass – and the traffic, eventually the police as well, be damned.

It was an instant holiday – SOMETHING HAD HAPPENED – and the American people took to the men of the convoy with a fervor generally reserved for major movie stars and glaringly unqualified presidential candidates. In each of the small towns and cities they passed through, the convoy received a welcome usually accorded a triumphant army liberating a town.

First would come the teenagers in their fantastic assortment of packed vehicles that ranged from Baja bugs to family Cadillacs, swooping out of the side roads to join the trucks for the procession through town. Then the signs and banners appeared, some of them stretching clear across the highway, all of them bearing slogans of welcome and support.

The main streets were two or three deep with spectators. There were the inevitable trucker groupies taking Instamatic photos of their heroes and begging for bits of clothing or hair. As Spider Mike passed the main intersection in Santa Rose, a hysterical teenage girl wrestled herself free from the grasp of her father and leaped on the running board to give him a big, sloppy, but undeniably enthusiastic kiss.

On the outskirts of town, Pig Pen was accosted by two young women on a motorscooter.

"Where you headed?" the blonde passenger called out as they pulled alongside. She was wearing shorts and a halter top.

Pig Pen sat up a little straighter and shrugged. "East. We might just end up in the Atlantic Ocean if we don't find somewhere better."

"Give us a ride," the brunette driver begged. She appeared to be a little bit taller and was wearing the top of a bikini and jeans.

Pig Pen shook his head no. He'd had enough of horny

young hitch-hikers for one day. Still the girls did look damn nice on that itty bitty scooter. And you really couldn't tell about a person from a bad time with another one.

"Say, how old are you girls?" he called down to them.

"I'm eighteen," the blonde answered. "And Linda here's almost twenty. Why?"

"Because I ain't givin no rides to minors," Pig Pen yelled back. "But you girls is different. Follow me off to the side up yonder."

Inside of five minutes, the go-go girls were grunting in some confusion at the motorbike that had joined them in back, while Linda and her friend Arliss were blowing their minds over Pig Pen's cab.

"Wow, it's a waterbed!" Linda squealed.

"Dig this far-out fur," Arliss purred, rubbing her bare back and shoulders against it in a way that made Pig Pen take something close to a death grip on the steering wheel.

"Were you with the convoy from the very beginning?" Linda wanted to know. By now both of the girls were stretched out in the sleeper, facing him and rocking gently with the rhythm of the road.

Pig Pen cleared his throat. "Was I there, darlin? Why you might say I *was* the beginnin of this here convoy, least as much as anybody else."

"Tell us about it," they cried in unison, leaning half out of the sleeper so as not to miss a word.

Pig Pen took it up a gear in order to catch up with the rest of the convoy. His grin was wide enough to drive an eighteen-wheeler through without touching the sides. Now this was more like what a convoy was supposed to be about. "Well, just this mornin over in Arizona, me and the Duck and Spider Mike was . . ."

At just about the city limits sign, a battered fifty-two Ford pulled up next to the Duck. In it were two sixtyish spinster sisters who had presided over the town's library, covered dish suppers, and ice cream socials since Hector was a pup. Mindy, the youngest by a year, held out a three level hamper toward the Duck's cab.

"I'm sorry, ladies, but I can't stop with all them trucks 'n people back there. But I sure do thank you now."

"God bless you, Rubber Duck," Mindy called back. She tossed a cookie in the direction of his open window, but it fell short on the pavement between them.

"Moa, don't you be wastin any more of that good food," the Duck said. "Your blessin is more than sufficient. And we're sure taking that along with us."

"Amen to that," Melissa commented as the old Ford fell back and disappeared on a side road. "I've got a feeling we're going to need all the blessing we can get."

The Duck looked straight ahead. "Ain't nothin stopped us yet. Ain't nothin going to either, less'n it's ourselves."

In the silence that followed, her glance fell on the gauges and meters of the instrument panel and she began to study them.

"I can figure out most of them," she said, "but what's that one for?"

The Duck laughed at her earnestness. "I guess that's one you wouldn't be likely to find on your average car. That's a pyrometer, tells you your exhaust temperature." His voice took on a warm, absorbed tone. "It's connected to a thermocouple in the exhaust system. You don't watch that gauge, first thing you know, you're up around 1,500 degrees and there goes a valve at least . . . you followin this?"

"More or less. You know, you really love this truck, don't you? I mean you know every little piece of it. Is that why you drive?"

The Duck considered that one for a moment.

"No," he said finally. "If it was, I'd be a mechanic. No, I like known how she works, but it's the driving itself." He started to grin. "And that's not about machinery – exactly. Come over here. Sit next to me."

Drawn by the challenge in his voice, Melissa slid over until the sides of their legs were touching.

"Put your hand on the wheel," he directed. Warily, she stretched out her right hand and grasped the warm, vibrating plastic. It moved under her fingers like a captured animal. The Duck smiled at the expression on her face. "Feel it?" he asked, knowing that she did. She nodded, either unwilling or unable to speak.

"That's eight hundred horsepower. Now grab it, take hold with your other hand, too."

Before she was really set, he let go of the wheel, leaving her in panic-stricken control. Suddenly she felt the power of it all, surging through her arms, her whole body. She fought to keep the truck, and herself, together and headed down the road.

"That's pure power," the Duck spoke quietly, very close to her but beyond her vision, which was focused on the road. "Forty tons of tractor and trailer. That's what you got in your hands. Eighty thousand pounds goin seventy miles an hour.

"Feels like you couldn't ever stop it, but you can. See that airbrake down there – don't touch it for goddamn's sake. If we didn't have that load and you hit that air too quick, she'd throw you right through the windshield. I've seen it happen, couple of times."

Melissa was gradually getting the feel of it. The cramped grip of her hands relaxed a bit. "Easy. That's right. Firm and easy," he encouraged her. He pressed on the accelerator and the motor noise began rising to a higher pitch.

"Listen to it." The Duck reached for the shift column. "Put your hand on mine."

As Melissa covered his shift hand with hers, he returned his free hand to the wheel to help with the steering.

"Twelfth gear," he explained. "There's thirteen. You got to double clutch each time. Feel the changes?"

Melissa nodded. "It's incredible. I don't know if I'm hearing it or feeling it."

"Both," he said seriously. "Kinda makes your bones hum, like ridin a race horse. And you're controlling all that power. You can make it respond." He took control of the wheel enough to make the big truck sway momentarily back and forth across the yellow line. Then he pulled it smoothly back on course. His voice took on a less professional tone.

"There's times, well it's like being one thing, me 'n this old kidney stomper. No difference at all. It's like I'm completely inside her, and I know what I can do, how far I can take her . . ."

His voice trailed off as the realization struck him – and a split second later, Melissa – that he was talking about a lot more than driving a truck. He gave a little laugh and touched her shoulder to break the tension between them.

"I guess you're followin this," he kidded.

Melissa didn't laugh, just kept on staring at him with eyes full of a hundred mysterious things. His smile disappeared.

"Good to have you aboard, man," he said with entire honesty.

She cocked her head just slightly in his direction.

"Good to be here," she answered in the same serious tone.

The frustrating enchantment of the moment was broken by the voice of Spider Mike on the CB. "Spider Mike calling Rubber Duck. Got a copy on me, man?"

"Go, Spider Mike," the Duck replied.

"Hey listen, I just got a skip from the home twenty and I'm a damn near daddy, man."

"That's not too bad either."

"Yes, congratulations," Melissa put in.

"Only it means I got to catch old Route 18 for Amarillo up the road here a piece," Spider Mike explained apologetically. "I'm gonna miss you guys."

"We're gonna miss your butt, too," the Duck assured him. "Maybe we'll catch you on the flip-flop, huh?"

"We love you, honey," the Widow Woman came in. "Don't forget your old Widow Woman, hear."

The reading of her novel had continued right along with a few major alterations. Since obviously she couldn't read and drive at the same time, it was decided unanimously by her audience, which by this time included even Big Nasty, that a relief driver from one of the other rigs would drive for her while she continued the book. As Pig Pen had put it for them all, "I just want to see whether that Errol ever gets anything offa her or not."

The relief man turned out to be a six-three two hundred and twenty pounder about the Widow Woman's age, who displayed all the manner and bearing of a mouse, a shyness he had acquired from having spent the bulk of his adult life and a good part of his youth behind the wheel.

"My handle's Badger Bob, mam," he said softly as he slid in behind the wheel. As soon as he started the truck in motion, it was obvious that he'd been born to it, so the Widow Woman relaxed into her book.

"You know, that's quite a book," he said when she paused at the end of the chapter.

"You really like it?" she asked, truly surprised.

"I surely do, mam. And I think the reader ain't so bad neither," he blurted out before he could stop himself.

The Widow Woman was touched, touched in an area that was all too familiar. It was happening again. "Why thank you, Badger Bob," she said. "You ain't married are you?"

He shook his head shyly, keeping his eyes straight ahead, "No mam, I surely ain't. Ain't been no call to up till now."

The Widow Woman smiled and moved a little closer on the seat.

" 'But where was Errol,' " she read. " 'Agatha's whole body ached with her need for him to feel the strength of his arms enveloping her.' "

"Ya hoo," Big Nasty broke in excitedly. "Go get it Errol, boy. Git after it man."

Suddenly a bank of blinding lights appeared beside the Duck's cab. It was the NBC van again.

"Them sons of bitches," he growled when he had gotten the truck and his heartbeat under control. "I've had just more'n enough of this particular weasel shit." Under the lights Dave Raymond could be seen talking excitedly to a TV camera.

His voice hesitated some when he noticed that the Duck had drifted over into their lane and was in the process of squeezing them off the road. He yelled "Cut!" and grabbed for his bullhorn.

"What are you doing, you shithead?" he screamed into the Duck's window, which by now was only inches from the van.

The Duck stuck his head out and said, "Just tryin to get up real close for the interview."

By this time, the van was running with one set of tires well off the pavement.

"You're crowding us off the road," Raymond shouted.

"Do tell. Well then I better pull her back over into my lane. What my suggestion is, is that you all do the same."

The big Mack began drifting back into the right lane.

"Wait a minute. You can't do that. You're big news,"

Raymond called after it. A single hand with the middle finger raised was extended from the window.

"Haven't you heard about the governor?" Raymond screamed in desperation as the Duck put the hammer down and began to pull away.

This time both of his hands appeared conveying the same message. Raymond was confused. Who was driving the truck? It couldn't be Melissa. That would be like a poodle tamer wrestling an elephant. He became aware of the pulsing red lights of the police cruiser just as the first blast of its siren caught him squarely between the ears.

The Duck, too, was startled by the sudden appearance of the cruiser and its motorcycle escort. Why had that news van showed up – to film the big bust? Then he noticed the man in the suit leaning out of the back window of the car and speaking into a bullhorn. The van had pulled ahead of both vehicles and was busily filming the action.

"Hello. Greetings Rubber Duck," the man called. 'Jesus Christ,' Arnoldi – for who else could it be? – thought to himself. 'What a klutz, and you've got all those cameras there, boy.'

The Duck didn't even look around, so Arnoldi plunged right on.

"I'm Chuck Arnoldi, Special Assistant to Governor Haskins. Can you stop? I'd like to talk with you."

The Duck looked over and shook his head no.

"I have a message from Governor Haskins," Arnoldi announced impressively.

The Duck shrugged. So what?

Arnoldi's exasperated glance fell on the TV van, which was still filming away, and he fell prey to a sudden inspiration. Inside, where he caged his most private emotions, he began to chuckle. It was perfect. Let U.P.I. get a shot of that and splash it all over the front pages.

"Then if you won't stop, can you slow down so I can climb on your running board and talk?" he called.

The Duck considered that for a while. The man was an asshole, but it might be fun to shake him up a little bit, especially in front of all those newspeople. Besides, it couldn't hurt to know in advance what the Governor thought he was up to. Slowing to about fifty, he motioned Arnoldi to come aboard.

The cruisier moved in closer and the transfer began. The back door of the car opened and slammed shut several times before the hold-open mechanism could control it. Arnoldi hunched himself up on the doorsill and extended a toe toward the truck's running board like a reluctant old maid testing the temperature of a swimming pool.

Then the Duck couldn't help himself. Just as Arnoldi's foot was about to make contact with the running board, the truck veered to the right, leaving him only the whistling slipstream for support. Through some truly heroic gyrations of his free arm, Arnoldi regained his equilibrium and had almost succeeded in pulling himself back into the cruiser when it ran smack into the middle of a big pothole in the road.

For a few desperate seconds, Arnoldi hung suspended from the swaying door. The cruiser started to brake, almost lost him completely when the door threatened to bounce shut, and resumed a constant speed.

The Assistant Director in the van put a hand on Raymond's shoulder.

"Jesus," he said worriedly, "maybe we ought to try to give him some help."

Raymond fixed him with a furious stare. "Roll em," he ordered. "This is a classic. We can't interfere."

When he sensed that Arnoldi had had enough, the Duck eased the van over so that his running board was only inches from the man's frantically scrambling heels.

"Step back," he commanded, leaning out to grasp Arnoldi's jacket. He tugged, Arnoldi threw himself against the cab door like a slightly overweight porpoise, and it was done.

"Well, well, pardner," the Duck said to the astounded, gasping face, "nice to have you aboard. That was some trick. Impressed the hell outta those news fellas."

At the mention of the media crew, an automatic smile wavered to the surface of Arnoldi's face. He had made it. And the TV cameras had recorded it all for generations of voters to come. Was still recording it, he reminded himself. He pulled himself together and launched into his presentation.

"First, on behalf of Governor Haskins, I would like to welcome you to our state." The Duck cocked an eyebrow without comment.

"As you may know, the Governor has long had an interest in the problems of the trucking industry," Arnoldi went on. "And so he has asked me to extend his personal invitation to you and your convoy to spend the night at the Tucumcari Municipal Park. As his guests, of course."

The Duck spoke then. "Horseshit," he said.

"No, no, it's true," Arnoldi persisted. "Governor Haskins wants to come out and meet with you, iron this whole thing out man to man. I made the arrangements for the park myself. You must be tired, aren't you?"

That was the trouble with bullshit, the Duck thought sourly. After a while it got to be insulting. Not so much what was being said as the fact that they expected you to be dumb enough to believe it. He was pissed.

"Get off my truck," he bellowed at the astounded Arnoldi.

'Jesus,' Arnoldi said to himself, 'this guy is really paranoid.' He wondered if all the others were the same. Aloud he said, "Look, I'm absolutely sincere. The police won't bother you. They have strict orders too . . ."

The Duck had pulled a crescent wrench from under the seat and laid it lightly across Arnoldi's knuckles. "Get off," he warned again in a quieter but more menacing voice.

Arnoldi couldn't allow this to happen. It would destroy the whole image he had so recently risked his life to create. It could ruin his political future for years to come. He decided on a desperate expedient – the truth.

"Okay, wait. I'll level with you. Can I level with you?"

The Duck set the wrench on the seat next to him. "Level with me."

"The Governor has been requested to call out the National Guard on you," Arnoldi explained. The rest of his statement was interrupted by a curve, which pinned him to the side of the cab as the truck roared around it. "Well anyway," he continued when they were back on the straight, "there's an election coming up, y'understand. And all those people that have been coming out to support you – they're voters."

The Duck nodded. Now this was beginning to make some sense he could understand.

"How's it going to look to them if the Governor tells the army to blow the shit out of your convoy, huh?"

"He's got a point."

The intrusion of a female voice led Arnoldi to attempt to make the speaker out in the soft glow from the instrument panel. She remained an intriguing shadow. He knew, as did anyone who listened to the radio or watched television that day, that her name was Melissa Dawes and that she was a well-known photo journalist. What she was doing with the convoy was anybody's guess, but it wasn't his problem.

"What does the Governor want with me?" the Duck was asking.

"Just to talk. Maybe he can help you. Maybe you can help him. One hand washes the other. You're trying to accomplish something by all this. He has the power to get things done."

"Sounds reasonable," the Duck agreed. He turned to Melissa. "What do you think?"

Melissa had her answer ready. Sometimes, later, Arnoldi would wonder if they had prepared it ahead of time.

"I think you ought to meet with the Governor," she said in a crisp voice, "on the condition, of course, that certain things are guaranteed in writing."

She ticked them off on her fingers to the bewildered Arnoldi. "Hands off truckers. No arrests. No harassment. And that includes no speeding tickets for under sixty-five as long as the convoy is in this state." She addressed the Duck. "Did I forget anything?"

"That about covers it."

Arnoldi was stunned, not so much by the demands – he'd anticipated all of them – as by the person presenting them. Who was the woman anyway? "I'm sure that the Governor would agree to such a guarantee," he promised weakly.

"In writing," the Duck prompted him.

"Fair enough. Uh, mam may I ask . . ."

"She's my legal advisor," the Duck interrupted and answered him. "Excuse us." He leaned over and whispered in Melissa's ear. She giggled and nodded.

"Well, I hope you don't take this personal, and it's not that I don't trust all you fine political fellas, but I'd like to guarantee that guarantee of the Governor's. So we're just gonna keep you with us for a while."

Suddenly he rolled up the window, catching Arholdi's left arm in a firm but painless grip. There was no way to pull free.

First, Arnoldi was terrified. Then simply panic-stricken. Finally, he was appalled, chagrined, humiliated. What kind of figure was this to cut on national TV? But wait. Something might still be saved.

"I'm a hostage," he called out to the ever-present cameras, leaning back to emphasize his imprisoned arm. "Tell the Governor to hurry. I'll hold out as long as I can."

"Hey y'all," Spider Mike came on the CB, "that's just about my turnoff up ahead. I'll be sayin goodbye."

After the general chorus of well-wishing had tapered off, the Duck came on.

"Hey man," he said in a serious voice, "you keep your eyes peeled, okay?"

"Roger, will do," Spider Mike answered cheerfully. "But there ain't gonna be any trouble, Duck. I'm just a poor boy on his way home to become a daddy, that's all. Case anybody asks, I don't know nothin about no convoy."

"Sounds like a plan," the Duck acknowledged. "But listen. Out there, you gotta be your own front door, and back door, too. Keep it cool."

"Ten-four on that. Ain't nothin goin to happen to me. I got friends in high places. Besides, we're heroes. Didn't you know that?"

"Okay." The Duck tried to laugh his sense of foreboding away. "You give that littleun our very best, hear. We'll be thinkin about ya."

"And I do thank you," Spider Mike said. "It's been a real trip, Duck. Anytime you got the front door, reserve me a place in your rockin chair." His old Diamond Reo pulled out of line at the next crossroads and headed south. When it had dwindled to a pair of distant taillights on the verge of becoming one, the Duck picked up the mike again.

"Listen, all you fellas," he announced, "I got a proposition for ya. The Governor of this here state wants to talk to us."

"Holy shit," somebody finally said out of the silence.

"What's he want?" another voice asked.

"Don't know for sure," the Duck answered truthfully. "But he sent his assistant all the way out here just to invite the convoy to stop over at the park outside of Tucumcari. We got a guarantee of no arrests – for speeding or anything. We also got his assistant sort of tied up here to back it up. He says we're the Governor's guests. Whaddya say?"

"Holy shit," a new voice said in the same hushed tone, "this is gonna be one hell of a party."

After the general uproar had subsided to a buzz, the Duck tried to break through again.

"Who we got on our back door?" He had to ask several times before the others quieted down to let him be heard.

"You got the Georgia Gator here," the answer came back, "and your ass is as safe as if it was restin in your momma's hands."

"A big ten-four on that, old buddy. You seen any signs of bears in that vicinity?"

"Negatory. She's clean all the way. Ain't seen it like this since the war. Looks like them Smokey's all went back to Ranger school."

"Ten-four, good buddy. And here's hopin they stay there."

"Positorily. Over and out."

But the Duck was still frowning as he clicked off the mike and hung it on the dash.

"What's wrong?" Melissa asked.

He shook his head as if to get a bad smell out of his nose. "Feels bad," he answered. He took a long look to the south. "I don't like anybody leavin the convoy. Not this soon. Not yet."

"I know what you mean," she agreed. "But I also had an Irish grandmother who used to tell me – 'Melissa don't borry trouble. There's always plenty enough around for free.' What do you say?"

The Duck relaxed a little, even smiled. "You know," he said appreciatively, "You're one hell of a woman."

She punched him lightly on the arm. "Holy shit," she said, chuckling as much to herself as him, "this is gonna be one hell of a party."

CHAPTER EIGHT

THERE was a reason for the absence of bears on the convoy's tail, or at least for the absence of the great big Papa Bear in sheep's clothing. Lyle was in jail. Suspicion of impersonating an officer, grand theft auto, and resisting arrest – Hamilton informed Fish as they sped toward the State Police substation where Lyle was locked up.

"What in hell happened?" Fish asked in amazement. "Old Lyle in the slammer?"

"Damned if I know," Hamilton replied. "The girl at the State Police switchboard said he was pretty incoherent – and horribly obscene."

"Well, at least we know we've got the right man. You know, when that call came in for us to go and spring the son of a bitch, I almost turned in my badge."

Hamilton nodded sympathetically. "Know what you mean," he agreed. "Know what you mean." A devilish grin began· spreading across his face. "Busted his ass," he chuckled. "What do you suppose he could have done?"

Fish laughed. "I can hardly wait to find out," he admitted. He checked his watch. "But on the other hand, I can't see where there's all that great a rush to see him again. What say we stop at that little diner up there for coffee?"

Hamilton caught on and slowed for the turnoff.

"Now that you mention it, there's no use charging into something before you're prepared."

Fish chuckled appreciatively. "I think I'll have a piece of pie. I hear they make them individually, from scratch."

What had happened was simple, at least as simple as things usually got for Lyle. His first clue that all might not be entirely well occurred as he rounded a curve at a conservative eighty-five, and his engine died. Deprived of acceleration to hold him on line – a little trick he had picked up by watching a Bill Bondurant TV special – Lyle shot across the opposite lane and halfway up a pretty steep embankment. When its momentum was spent, the car began slipping backward, finally arriving back at the road with a thump that deposited Lyle in the rear seat.

He gathered himself together, crawled out of the door with a little less assurance than he generally liked to show in public, and wobbled to the hood to check things out. Everything looked fine. He got back in the car and cranked her up. Beyond a first few feeble attempts to catch, the motor just sat there like the lump of shit Lyle knew it to be. Before he had completely loosened the wing nut on the carburetor, he realized what was wrong. It had to be. It was too fucking damnedably perfect.

He reached in the front window and turned the key to 'on'. The needle on the temperature gauge rose up to almost off the scale; the needle on the alternator gauge moved slightly to the minus side to acknowledge the operation of the temperature gauge; the needle on the gas gauge just sat there deader'n a fuckin doorknob. Jesus Christ, he was out of gas!

He thought of looking for a reserve can in the trunk until he remembered that in his haste of getting out of Allington, he'd taken only the ignition key which, naturally, didn't fit the trunk.

He thought of flagging down a car until he noticed the deserted highway, he thought of walking for gas until he noticed that there was no man-made light to be seen within the visible horizon; he thought of fuckin killing himself until he noticed the headlights of a GOD DAMNED CAR! coming at him from the west. He ran to the center of the lane and stood there with arms outstretched. He'd stop the sons of bitches if it meant his life.

It almost did. The headlights didn't slow at one hundred yards, or fifty. When the oncoming vehicle was twenty-five yards away and still doing its original seventy, seventy-five, Lyle began jumping up and down and waving his arms like a cheerleader. At the last split-second, he made a spinning backdive into the ditch.

He came up choking cursing, covered with dust. He

brushed himself off as best he could only to discover some kind of shit garbage stuck on unbrushably to the seat of his pants. Goddamn, you never could trust a man that would buy one of them little foreign cars anyways. He'd settle with that son of a bitch later. What to do now was the problem. For probably the twentieth time that day, Lyle regretted changing from his uniform to civies before he left Allington. Camouflage be damned – a man wasn't safe on the roads these days without some kind of uniform.

The next set of lights appeared about twenty-five minutes later. They belonged to an ancient Peterbilt log truck, which pulled over and stopped when Lyle signaled, this time a little more realistically, from the shoulder of the road. The driver, whose handle turned out to be Dusty Dan, was a weathered, bearded old man who gave the impression that his company had taken the toughest, strongest tree trunk from the load in back and propped it up in the driver's seat.

"Ran out of gas," Lyle explained, his foot already on the running board. "How about a ride?"

Dusty Dan nodded him in and started the truck rolling before the door was completely closed. Within a half a minute, he had it movin right along about seventy-five to the accompaniment of every loose bolt, hinge and piece of metal in the cab. The effect was something like taking a carnival ride through the percussion section of a symphony orchestra.

"Bad place to run out of gas," he bellowed after they had hurtled through about five miles of nothing but sagebrush and jackrabbits.

"You tellin me? You're the second person drove by in a half hour."

"Wouldn't a been me either if it wasn't for this here convoy. You heard about it? It's all in the news."

Lyle nodded. "What's that got to do with it?" he asked cautiously. Something warned him that this man wasn't his friend, or sure as hell wouldn't be if he found out who he was.

"Gonna join up," Dusty Dan answered as if it was the most obvious thing in the world. "I don't have to get these here logs into Amarilla till tomorrow night sometime. But the way I see it, them fellas is doin somethin ought to have been done years ago, and they'll need all the help they can get."

"Specially when they all get their asses busted sooner or later," Lyle ventured, trying not to be any more of a non-entity than he absolutely had to.

Dusty Dan gave him a hard look and slowed down to where he could be heard over the conglomeration of clanks and rattles in the cab.

"You ain't of them Smokey-lovers, are ya?" he demanded accusingly.

"Me? Course not. I hate the bastards."

"Well, that's good," Dusty Dan went on relieved. "Cause I don't mind tellin ya they ain't no room for Smokies *or* Smokey-lovers in this here cab. I wouldn't give a one of them fuckers the sweat off my balls."

"Say, exactly what distance we talkin about to this gas station?" Lyle asked nervously as they flashed past another set of unlit pumps.

Dusty Dan threw a glance at the instrument panel. "I make it just about 11.8 miles. Only station that's open this time of a Sunday night twixt here and Tucumcari."

Lyle sat back and prepared to shut up. This was another bastard he'd take care of on the way back if need be. He was getting himself quite a list, but he wasn't the kind of man to forget anything or anybody on it.

"What do you think about that there convoy?" Dusty Dan asked in a tone of voice that left little doubt as to what Lyle was supposed to think about it.

"They sure are doin somethin," he said neutrally, hoping it would pass. It didn't. Dusty Dan fixed him with an angry glare.

"Somethin!" he exploded. "I'll say they're doin somethin. It's about time some of us got to kick a little ass stead of just taken it. What do ya think of that chickenshit cop that started the whole thing?"

"Who was that?" Lyle asked innocently.

"Aw, that turd Wallace over in Arizona. I been hearin stories about that particular piece of turkey shit for years. The way I heared it, he's one of them guys that could walk under a snake's belly with his hat on."

"Well, as I understand it, they was speedin when he got em the first time," Lyle defended himself in absentia.

"Entrapment. That's the way that bastard works. You can bet your wife's pussy on that. Naw, that sucker's a real bastard," Dusty Dan concluded, looking to Lyle for confirmation.

"Yeah," Lyle answered without a lot of conviction.

"A real turkey turd," Dan went on, still looking at him.

"Sure is," Lyle agreed. Jesus, another couple of minutes of this and he'd begin to believe it himself. He fingered the badge in his pocket for security.

"Well, I'll tell you this. I been a trucker most all of my life, and I know for a fact that if we ever catch that son of a bitch when he ain't hidin behind his badge, they's a bunch of us gonna stomp his ass."

They rode in silence for maybe ten seconds.

"What line of work did you say you was in?" Dan asked, trying to remember.

"Travelin," Lyle answered quickly. "Right now you might say I'm travelin."

Dan nodded his head. "Sort of a salesman, huh?"

"You might say that," Lyle answered, mentally adding Dusty Dan's name to his get-em-on-the-flip-flop list.

They rounded a curve and a cluster of lights sprang into view ahead on the right.

"There's your station," Dan said. He hit the brakes and pulled to a stop on the apron.

"Much obliged," Lyle said as he climbed out of the vibrating door with more than common relief.

"Don't mention it. Good luck on gettin a ride back," Dusty Dan answered. "if worse comes to worse, there's a Greyhound stops here in about ..." he checked his watch, "... three and a half hours. Well, I'm gonna have ta get the hammer down if I'm gonna catch up with that convoy while it'll still do some good."

After the truck had clanked and rattled out of sight, Lyle started walking up to the station. One thing was for damn sure – he wasn't waiting three and a half hours for no damn bus. He automatically reached for his wallet before he remembered it wasn't there. Then he pulled out his badge and pinned it on his shirt pocket. By God, he was on the side of the Law. And it was goddamn past time for him to be getting a little respect.

Which, oddly enough, was the subject of a conversation between Governor Haskins and his one remaining aide back at the mansion. They had just viewed the first newsclips of the Arnoldi Fiasco, complete with shots of Arnoldi exhibiting his imprisoned arm and vowing to hang on to the end.

"Humph," Big Hank grumbled. "Fine respect for law and order. That's your truckers for you."

Haskins laughed and said, "Henry, all those years of political experience have robbed you of your sense of humor. Don't you see the absolute appropriateness of it all?"

Big Hank continued frowning for a moment and then, despite himself, began to smile. The smile turned to a chuckle which in turn became an uncontrollable burst of hysterical laugher. Haskins joined in.

"I can't say I haven't had the urge to try something like that myself from time to time," Big Hank said. "Maybe this will teach that young puppy a lesson."

"Which particular one did you have in mind?"

Big Hank bent forward and caught the younger man's glance with a pointed look. "That if you put your finger in the cookie jar, somebody's liable to close the lid on you."

"Henry, I really want to try this," Haskins replied seriously. "I think it might do some good."

"It's political dynamite."

The Governor put his hand on the older man's shoulder. "I know you're right, Henry," he said, "and that someday soon I'll have to come to realize that or get out of politics. But, for now, before that day comes, let me have a fling or two at really representing the people, okay?"

Big Hank shook his head. His expression revealed a mixture of both admiration and despair.

"You'll regret it," he predicted solemnly. "It just doesn't make any sense. Not in this world."

It was about three-quarters of an hour later that Willy Johnson was on the tow truck CB to the State Police. A skinny little man in his middle forties, Willy seemed to have been created to provide comic relief for Don Knotts, and practically everybody else he met. He had taken the job as night attendant at the Severn's Crossing Mobil station because his wife had threatened to put him out of the house if he didn't do something besides play solitaire and watch TV all day.

"Honest, Sergeant," he was saying, "that's exactly how she happened. I was just sittin there mindin the station like always when this big log truck pulls in and drops this feller off. What? No, I don't think the truck driver was in on it. Probably just gave him a lift.

"Well anyways, this feller walks up to me cool as you please and says he run out of gas up the road a piece. So I says, 'How much you want?' And he says, 'Couple of gallons.' And I says, 'You got to leave a five dollar deposit less'n you got your own can.' That's company policy, ya know.

"Well, then he points to this badge he's got pinned to his pocket and says he's a police officer and this is an emergency . . . Nope, I didn't see what it was exactly, but it weren't no New Mexico shield cause I know what they look like. Listen, Sergeant, he was a pretty big guy. I wasn't about to mess with him if I didn't have to.

"When I give him the gas, he says, 'Now you're gonna give me a ride back to my car.' Well I says, 'Can't do that. It's against the company rules,' but that didn't bother him none. He just points to that badge again and says for me to get my ass in gear. Them bastards was gonna be out of the state before he could catch up with them. Yeah, that's his exact words – 'Them bastards gonna be out of the state before I can catch up with them.'

"So, I drove him out to his car in the tow truck. Yeah, it was a white Plymouth, sort of ivory. The back license plate was all bent down like it had been in a wreck so's you couldn't read it. He put in the gas, spilled about half the can, and took off like a bat out of hell goin east.

"Yeah, there was one other thing that was kinda strange. I had the radio in the truck on and there was this news bulletin, you know, about the Governor meeting with them truckers in Tucumcari. Well, that seemed to get him real upset, real upset. He was just cursin and carryin on after that ...

"Wait a minute. I'm just back at the station now and the lock on one of the pumps is broke. Musta been him. No, I can't prove it, but he couldn't get very far with the gas he had, and he was headin this way. Why don't you tell whoever comes out here to get some fingerprints ...

"You mean to tell me that *all* your men's tied up with that convoy? Well, that's a fine damn thing ... Yeah, I'm sure you'll keep your eye on it. Sure. By the way Sergeant, if you do catch that fella, do me a favor and give him one up side the head for me. He's about the most ornery, miserable cuss I ever run acrost."

The most ornery, miserable cuss just about anybody had ever seen at this point was burning up the road, on the verge of making a decision. Ever since he'd heard that news report about the Governor meeting with the truckers, Lyle had realized that his hours as a potential hero were numbered. He knew what was too often the result of those kinds of negotiation – amnesty.

The word stuck in his guts like a half-digested chile rellano. If those damn truckers got off scot free, then he, of all the people who had tried to apprehend them, would come out looking like a perfect asshole. Lyle wasn't about to let that happen if he could prevent it some way. At least if it came to that, he wanted a few cracks at some of those sons of bitches before they were turned into model citizens.

Of course he might attract more attention than he wanted this way, and there was always the possibility that he could get killed if he ran into anybody not fast enough to get out of his way, a danger made even more probable by the fact that the sandstorm had disabled his siren. But none of that mattered now. It was time to act.

He passed the *Wilbur, Pop. 2800, Speed Limit 35* sign with a sneer. He even pushed the accelerator pedal closer to the floor. With one hand jammed on the horn, Lyle tore through the center of town at a cool 93.5 miles per hour. Which, needless to say, woke up a lot of people, including one elderly gentleman who rushed from his house to see what the hell was going on and came close to being the first traffic fatality of Lyle's career.

The village constable was one of those awakened, first by the horn itself and shortly thereafter by a series of irate telephone calls from his constituency. He grumbled dutifully at his wife and then called the State Police.

"Hello, Carl. This is Jim Lindquist over in Wilbur. I got a lot of complaints about this nut driving through the center of town at a hundred miles an hour, blowing his horn full blast the whole way ... Yeah, I know you're shorthanded, but I just thought you oughtta know ... One of the people who called said it was a white Dodge or Plymouth. Back plate seemed to be disguised or missing ... What's that? You think you got something on the driver? Good, good. Broke into a filling station back in Severn's Corners, eh? Kidnapped the attendant? Sounds like some rough customer. If he shows up around here again, I'll give you a call right quick."

Meanwhile on the outskirts of town Lyle was having his own troubles. Either from anger, relief at having made it through the town, or sheer exhaustion, he had missed the turn by the Masonic Temple and plowed across the lawn and halfway up of the porch of the building next door.

A man in a bathrobe helped him out from behind the wheel.

"What in the hell do you think you're doin, Jack?" he demanded as soon as he had Lyle shakily propped up against the car.

"Police officer," Lyle croaked, pointing to the badge still pinned to his pocket. "I'm on special assignment."

"What's going on out there, Harry," Called a whining female voice from just inside the front door.

Harry made an angry gesture toward the house. "Stay inside the house, Myrtle," he half-snarled, half-commanded. "Everything's all right. I'll handle this."

He turned back to Lyle. "Listen, Jack. I suppose you know you've caused considerable physical damage to my house, not to mention the peace of mind of my wife and myself," he said sternly.

But what took Lyle's attention was the wristwatch strapped to the man's arm. Jesus Christ, it was getting close to time for that conference and here he was still a good fifty miles away. He leaped back into the car and turned the ignition key. Miraculously the engine turned over and started. Lyle threw it into reverse and backed off the porch onto the lawn, ripping out an additional piece of railing in the process. "Can't stop to explain," he yelled to an astonished Harry. "Read the papers tomorrow, you'll understand."

The car roared out of the yard, leaving two deeply gouged tire marks as momentoes of the occasion . . .

"Yes, sir. We've had complaints on him earlier in the evening. We'll get right on it."

"Jesus," the duty officer said to the Lieutenant who'd been called in after the second complaint, "now he's running into houses."

"What?"

"I just had a call from a man in Wilbur. It seems that whoever he is drove through a hedge, across a lawn, and up onto the porch of this guy's home. It's the same guy – out of state badge and everything."

"Put out a bulletin to every car in the area to be on the lookout for this maniac. That goddamn convoy is trouble enough for one night. I want this other lunatic stopped – fast before those damn reporters get hold of it and the idea starts catching on."

They caught up with him in Victor, a tiny dot on the map east of Tucumcari. It was a doubleheader with one State Patrol car in front and one in the rear. The two Patrolman approached Lyle's door from opposite directions.

"Step out of the car, please," the one from in front said. Both of them had their pistols loosened in their holsters. Lyle got out.

"Now just a minute, you fellas . . ." He started to protest.

"Turn around and put your hands on the car please," the one behind him interrupted.

"Now just a damn minute, here." Lyle was starting to get real upset with these two. They were treating him just like a damn criminal. "Take a look at this," he demanded, punching his badge with an angry finger.

"Cover him, Jack," the first patrolman said. He came

closer and focused his flashlight on Lyle's pocket. "That's an Arizona badge," he declared after a close inspection that seemed to take forever.

"Course it is," Lyle said, having decided that only the truth could save him now. "Cause I'm an Arizona Sheriff. I'm Lyle Wallace. You heard about me on TV. I been chasing that convoy all the way from Arizona."

"Ah, do you have some identification, Mr. Wallace?" The one behind him asked in an altered tone, obviously impressed.

"Well, that's the hang of it. I ran into these two fellas back around Santa Rosa who pulled me out of the ditch and then turned a knife on me and took my wallet. Money, driver's license, everything."

"So you have no identification except that badge? Is that what your telling us?"

"No, but you can call the Chief in Allington. That's where I got this car. And there are those two FBI men. They can tell you who I am."

"FBI men?"

"Yeah, two of them. One's name is Hamilton. Forgot the other's. After we went up in the copter they took off for Santa Fé."

The two patrolmen looked at each other. Lyle was interesting but enough was enough.

"Mr. Wallace, I'm afraid you'll have to come along with us. We'll get this all straightened out back at the station."

"You mean, you're arrestin me."

"Let's just say we'd like you to come with us."

"Well, I ain't goin," Lyle grunted. "I ain't got the time."

And so the fight began. Lyle was experienced enough in police tactics to anticipate the assault from behind and elbow that patrolman back against the car. What he didn't expect was the reaction of the man's partner, who buried his fist in Lyle's midriff before the other officer even hit the ground. Then he pulled the gasping Lyle's hands behind his back and applied the cuffs. The battle was over.

"When the FBI hears about this, you're gonna be sorry," Lyle warned when he finally got his breath back.

"Sure, buddy. Sure," the patrolman who was riding in the

back seat with him said. "I've got to hand it to you though. That was quite a story you gave us. Almost had me believing it for a while."

It seemed like hours to Lyle before the cellblock door opened. The two FBI men and a State Police Captain came through it and walked over to Lyle's cell.

"Well, well, Lyle," Hamilton said jovially. "We do find you in the damndest places."

"Quite a list of charges they've got on you," Fish put in. "You've been busy."

"Are you two monkeys gonna get me outta here, or stand there and flap your jaws all night," Lyle growled.

"I suppose this is the man," the Captain sighed. He'd had hopes of keeping Lyle locked up for at least the rest of the night.

Hamilton nodded.

"Unlock it, Sergeant," the Captain said to another officer who had come in carrying a ring of keys.

"Thanks a bunch," Lyle snarled at the three men. "What did you guys do, stop for coffee?"

Hamilton and Fish carefully avoided each other's eyes to keep from breaking up. The Captain headed for the door. "He's all yours," he said to the two agents. "And you're welcome to him."

Outside as they waited for what was left of Lyle's car to be brought up from the police garage, Hamilton turned to him.

"You know, Lyle," he said conversationally, "you're a lucky son of a bitch. Since you did get yourself deputized in Allington, they had to drop the charges on you, provided there are no further incidents."

"You may have to pay for that house you demolished back in Wilbur," Fish added helpfully. "They're still negotiating that."

"Listen, you two wiseasses, by the time I get through with that convoy, this state will be buildin me a monument. You two pussies better just stand out of the way so's you don't get hurt."

Just then the car appeared in the entrance way to the underground garage. Lyle was sliding into the driver's seat before the patrolman driving it was all the way out. He pulled to a stop beside Hamilton and Fish.

"So long, Pussies. You know the trouble with you guys is that you got your heads so far up your asses, you don't even know what you're doin anymore."

"And I suppose you do," Hamilton challenged humorously.

"Listen, there's one difference between me and you two jerks – I got a plan."

With that Lyle stood on it and roared out of sight in a cloud of dust and burning rubber.

"Do you think he could really have a plan?" Hamilton asked.

"Let's hope not," Fish answered glumly. "I've got a feeling that our side is going to need all the breaks it can get."

A half hour later as he approached Tucumcari, Lyle was still pondering what that plan might be. He pulled into a crossroad diner outside of town to give himself a breather and figure out just what the hell he was going to do now that he was almost there.

A skinny teenager who looked as though he'd been dragged through the french fry machine was on counter duty for the night. "Heard about the convoy?" he asked cheerfully as he brought Lyle's order of coffee, black. "They went right by here a while ago."

"Yeah?" The kid was an asshole, but sometimes you got a lot of valuable information from assholes.

"I seen the Rubber Duck," the kid continued. He was obviously preparing for a new career as professional witness. "And I seen the lady with him. And you know that one they call Spider Mike? He pulled off right on the apron out there and then he headed south."

All the alarm bells in Lyle's sinking circuitry went off at once. "He what?" he asked incredulously.

"It's because his wife is having a baby. I heard it on the CB when they was passin by."

"What kind of truck was he drivin?"

"It was a Diamond Reo an old one. Couldn't see what he was haulin in the box though."

Lyle thought back to that morning, the highway, the

three trucks. It was Spider Mike all right. He made a dash for the door.

"Hey, mister," the counterman called after him, "you didn't drink your coffee."

"That's okay," Lyle called back through the closing door. "I ain't payin for it either."

Once outside, he ran to his car and pulled the New Mexico map from the glove compartment. He studied it intently, checked, double checked, checked it one more time to be absolutely sure. Then he allowed himself a truly evil laugh. There was no mistake. It was almost perfect.

He hurried to the pay phone out by the highway and used his last dime to make a long distance collect call.

"Hello, Tiny, this is Lyle Wallace ... yeah, it is a long time. Well, I'm over here near Tucumcari ridin herd on that convoy ... Yeah, they are a bunch of shitkickers for sure. But listen, I just got some pretty reliable word that one of the ringleaders is headin your way ... honest to God, his wife's havin a baby over there somewhere. His handle is Spider Mike and he should be gettin to your place within the next hour. He's drivin an old beat up Diamond Reo. You can't miss it ... It sure is a laugh ... But listen, if you bust him, you're in for some publicity, boy ... Forget about the goddamn amnesty. You're in Texas, that's a whole other state ... Course I'll pull up the backdoor on him, but with that wife of his set to pop any minute he ain't likely to be draggin his heels between here and there ... We got us our pigeon. All you got to do is hold the coop door open and close it behind him nice and tight."

After he hung up, Lyle walked back to his car, reflecting that he'd spring the rest of his plan on Tiny when the big guy was a little more ready for it. They had their pigeon all right, but they also had something else – the almost perfect irresistible bait.

CHAPTER NINE

IT was one hell of a party. The Duck and Melissa dropped Arnoldi at a service station out of town and then led a parade of trucks plus local vehicles to the municipal park. Once there, the convoy spread into small one or two vehicle units among the fire pits, tennis courts and softball diamonds. By the time the last truck had pulled in the park was full.

The Duck turned off the ignition and simply sat watching the convoy disperse around him. The insulation of the long hours on the road had begun wearing off as they approached Tucumcari, and for the past half hour he and Melissa had not spoken to each other except briefly about where to release Arnoldi. Real life, with all of its hassles and temptations was starting to break in.

"Well, let's hope the Governor really has something to offer," Melissa said finally to breach the silence that was growing into a wall between them.

When the Duck spoke, his voice was quiet, thoughtful. "He'd better. Whether anybody knows it or not, this convoy is over."

"What do you mean?" Melissa was completely taken off guard. How could he say something like that when they were surrounded by a parkful of trucks just waiting on his command?

In answer, he pointed to the scene spreading before them. A few scattered fires had been lit and more were in the works. Cases of beer, some of them donated by local markets and liquor stores, were strewn around the grounds like oversize confetti. Over by the wading pool a fight that had been brewing for the past fifty miles over the CB was beginning to take form.

"It's the end of the line," the Duck said flatly. "There's just a bunch of separate people out there."

Melissa felt a lump growing in her throat. Now that she saw what he meant, she didn't want it to be over, not this way. A couple of the Satans Mothers passed by, casually offering bong hits of angel dust to whoever was interested.

"And of the line for us, too, I reckon," the Duck said even more softly. As if to underline his point, an ABC news van pulled up next to the truck and began setting up lights and cameras.

"It doesn't have to be . . . any of that," Melissa choked out, wondering as she heard herself, exactly what she was trying to say.

The Duck smiled, the kind of wry smile that hurts. "You gonna write me every week?" he asked, mocking himself as well as her. "Maybe you could be my relief driver. Take pictures of all the truck stops between nowhere and nowhere else. Think you'd be happy with that?"

Melissa shook her head. The pain in her chest, which she could tell he was feeling too, told her it was all wrong, but he was right.

"So what do we do now?" she asked with a painful cheerfulness that about summed up the way she felt.

"I got to get out there and move around – see who's here and try to keep things from gettin too much out of hand."

"I thought you didn't want any responsibility for this," she challenged, trying to get out at least some of the sting of their separation. "Don't I recall you saying that everybody was following you because you were in front – and that was all there was to it?"

He nodded reluctantly. "Somebody's got to do it," he answered simply. "I don't see any takers right at the present time, so I guess it's me."

Melissa looked at him studying the tired lines around his mouth and eyes. What he said was true. He didn't want the power they had given him, but he'd accept it if there was no other way. She put a hand on his arm.

"You know, I've never known anybody like you. You're one hell of a man."

He put his arm around her and kissed her then. His lips were gentle on hers with a definite undertone of tightly controlled passion. At just the right moment, he let her go.

"And you're one hell of a woman." He chuckled to himself. "For a female picture taker."

"Female picture taker. I like that."

He studied her body briefly from across the distance of the seat. "So do I," he said seriously. A sudden outburst of angry voices pulled their attention to the wading pool, where the original fight was turning into a small scale riot with seven or eight truckers wrestling around in the foot deep water trying to clobber each other. The Duck sighed and reached for the door.

"I better get over there before they get out the tire irons," he said, his voice already assuming the tone of command he didn't want. "You can leave your stuff in the sleeper until you make arrangements with your friends. I'll see you before we leave, maybe."

Melissa smiled. However noble he was being, he wasn't through with her yet. "You can count on it," she said.

She remained in her seat while he walked over to the pool and sized things up. Then he waded out into the middle of it, grabbed the original combatants by the backs of their collars and pushed their heads under water. After fifteen seconds or so, he let them up to breathe. Within five minutes both sides were drinking together, pouring beer over each other's heads, and having one hell of a good time.

Melissa unlatched one of the suitcases in the sleeper and took out a towel. She'd noticed a shower building across the campground, and feeling that she'd been sitting in the dust and heat of the cab for at least a month, decided to head for it. Besides, her reporter's instinct told her there were a hundred stories going on out there. She'd more or less promised she'd take no pictures for sale, but nobody could expect her to turn off her eyes and ears.

In the few short minutes since their arrival, the camp had turned into a combination picnic, orgy and multiple ring circus.

The first group she ran across were the Satans Mothers, who had been reenforced by a half dozen of the Disciples, a local biker club. Between the angel dust and the beer, they were, to a man, totally wasted. Next to their huge bonfire, they had built a ramp of packing cases and planks ripped off the Little League bleachers, and were taking turns leaping the flames on their bikes.

As Melissa watched, one of the locals misjudged the ramp and crashed squarely in the middle of the fire. The bike skidded through the flames, scattering logs and ashes and finally plowing to a halt only inches from one of the Slaves and a local beauty who were locked in each other's arms and legs, and didn't appear to notice. The driver rolled out the other side with his leathers smoking. His friends gathered around in a circle whooping it up and using their beer bottles as extinguishers. After about half a minute of this, the Victim rolled over and took a hit on the nearest bottle.

"Hey, Evel?" one of his friends shrieked, at least partly with relief, "what do you do for an encore?"

The man staggered to his feet, righted his bike and fired her up. "I'm gonna make that sucker this time," he promised to a general chorus of All-rights and Go-for-its. Melissa turned away from the cheering voices and moved on. She really didn't want to see the outcome of that particular scene.

A little further on she came to an enormous house trailer of somewhat shady repute that had been rented by a hastily formed consortium of local ladies for the avowed purpose of cleaning up while the getting was good. A crude, hand-lettered sign attached to its side said simply *Come and Get It.* The first two truckers in the line outside were arguing over who was next. Suddenly Big Nasty stepped out of sixth place and marched up to them.

"Listen, boy," he rumbled, planting himself between them, "this ain't no way to be. After all, everybody's brothers here, ain't they?"

"But I was here first," Sad Sam, a little round trucker who came up to about Big Nasty's belt buckle complained. "The lady inside said I was next."

"The hell she did," the other man who was maybe an inch taller retorted.

"Tell you what I'll do if you two will stop your yammerin' for a minute," Big Nasty offered. He plunked himself on the chest with a size thirteen finger. "I'll decide, how's that?"

The two men looked up at Big Nasty's six-foot-five of solid

muscle and allowed how that seemed fair. Big Nasty stepped in front of both of them.

"What I decided," he announced, "is that I'm next. Now there ain't nothin to fight about, is there? Less'n of course you want to git into it with me."

"What the hell, I been waiting a month for somethin like this. I guess another fifteen minutes ain't gonna make no difference," Sad Sam said resignedly.

"I'll get behind you," the other man offered. "If you've got to wait fifteen minutes, I know I ain't gonna be out here more'n eighteen or twenty."

All over the campground various other contests had been shaping up. A slalom course had been set up on the soccer field and several of the truckers wheeled and fired their big rigs around it while others timed them on their digital chronographs.

Over on the softball field, a big GMC General and a Mack were having a tug of war across home plate. Large betting contingents had formed on either side of the twenty foot section of chain that connected the trucks rear to rear. The engines roared, tires spun, gouging great trenches into the infield. After what seemed a full minute of standoff, the Mack began pulling ahead, dragging the GMC inch by torturous inch across the on-deck circle, the batter's box. The spinning rear wheels of the GMC finally caught the edge of home plate, ripping it from the ground and sending it flying into the crowd. The match, except for the inevitable excuses and instant replays, was over.

On the entrance road, two tractors were lined up gunning their engines like hot rodders at a traffic light. Between them stood another example of the local talent, an oversized blonde who was holding her bra in her hand as the starting flag.

"On your mark, get set," she called twirling the bra above her head and doing a little dance, which did nothing to detract from the view. "One for the money, two for the show, three . . ."

"Just say Go, you dumb broad," growled one of the drivers.

"Don't call me a dumb broad," she replied in a huff. She

dropped her hands to her hips in indignation. "I'll say Go, when I . . ."

The rest of her declaration was lost in a cloud of dust as the two tractors peeled out hell-bent for the refreshment stand.

Melissa dodged the fuel tanker that was thoughtfully going from truck to truck, at a cool ten cents a gallon over the going price, and came across another equally bizarre but somehow appropriate scene. An NBC news crew had set up to shoot against the blank wall of the restroom building. It took Melissa a few seconds to realize that this would provide a neutral background over which clips of the camp could be dubbed for the actual broadcast.

Standing in front of the cameras and talking to them earnestly was none other than Dave Raymond. His appearance had changed somewhat since their last meeting on the road. He was now wearing a network blazer and had obviously received a hasty but respectable makeup job.

"There are more than just trucks involved now," he intoned in his best Walter Cronkite manner. "Private automobiles equipped with Citizens Band radios have joined. Our reporters have counted a wide variety of vehicles including out-of-service Greyhound bus, the touring van of the Sagebrush Corral – an area country-western band, a traveling fire and brimstone preacher in his gospel truck. They're all gathered here in the municipal park now, awaiting the arrival of the Governor. No one seems to know or particularly care what the outcome of these historic negotiations will be. A carnival atmosphere pervades the grounds, strangely reminiscent of the frantic gaiety of a 1930s Germany. One thing is certain – the convoy is here and it is here to stay, at least until its leaders arrive at some kind of settlement with the Governor. What or when that will be is still anybody's guess. This is Dave Raymond, NBC News, in Tucumcari."

He handed the mike to an assistant and hurried over to the edge of the crowd where he had spotted Melissa.

"How do you like it?" he asked, pointing to the blazer.

Melissa gave him an ironically appreciative whistle. "Big time."

"Special assignment from the network. You know what this means?" He began to sing, "New York City, here I come."

"I'm really happy for you, Dave," Melissa said seriously. "I know you've paid your dues."

"You can say that again. I've worked in towns so jerk-water that the people who lived there never heard of them. But how about you? What've you got for me?"

"Well, look Dave, it's not exactly what you think."

"I spoke to the networks. They went crazy when they heard you were working inside on this," he broke in, not really listening to her. "They want to send a plane to pick up your film."

"I'm not working, Dave." She reached into her carry bag and handed him the Nikon, empty.

"You're not working," he repeated, dazed. Then his face lit up with anger. "Yeah, yeah. Sure. Now I get it. *Paris Match* is sending a Concorde for your stuff. Dirty pool, Melissa. Not fair at all."

She shook her head. "It's not that, Dave. Nobody's getting anything from me. I threw the film away."

"Why would you . . . oho, aha, I see. Love at last. Cute, Melissa. Really charming. You're going to settle down outside of Memphis and raise baby diesels." His voice had grown progressively harsh, cynical. "Or can I say you and the Rubber Duck are just good friends? Can I announce your retirement?"

"Dave, it's a lot more simple than that. The man did me a favor. That isn't the way I return favors."

" 'The man did me a favor,' " he mimicked savagely. "And what about me? I'm offering to put you on top of the publishing world. Is that a favor?"

She shook her head slowly. "It is, but it's not enough."

"Enough? What would you know about enough?" His eyes, barely inches away, burned into her with an anger that could only be real. "When you were attending Bryn Mawr, or whatever finishing school you went to, I was getting up at five o'clock every morning to do the livestock quotations and weather in Mason City, Iowa. When your first big spread appeared in *Cosmo*, yours truly had worked himself all the way up to livestock quotations, weather *and* local news on the weekends. Get the point? This is *my* big break baby and I'm not going to let yours or anybody's overactive glands blow it for me."

"I'm sorry, Dave. There's nothing I can do."

"Nothing? You haven't been thinking, baby. You've been playing around in that cab too long. You know the score. Right now, old Lover Duck is a hero, because that's news, because *we* made him that way. This was just a police action until we came into it. And we can break him just as easy. Bang-bang, and they're closing the doors on him for a cool five to twenty. I'll tell you this – unless I get some cooperation from you, I'm going to start interviewing the cops."

Melissa took a long moment to decide. What Dave was telling her was rotten, but it was also true, a truth that was bred into anyone who had ever been near the business. It was news that mattered and for the media, truth was the most entertaining way of looking at it.

"So what do you want from me?"

"Anything. Background, personal observations. Right now I'm running out of material – I'll even take an exclusive interview."

She hesitated.

"Listen, you'll be doing him the biggest favor of his life," he went on convincingly. "I've seen the list of charges they've got stacked up on him, and I can tell you people have been hung in this country for less. Just because the Governor's making a big play coming down here doesn't guarantee anybody's getting off. You know politicians. It could just as easily go the other way if the wind changes. But you give me something to work with on your boy, something that's *news*, and we'll build him up so the President wouldn't dare touch a hair on his hallowed head. What do you say?"

"There are some tapes," she said hesitantly.

"Tapes. Yeah, that's good. What kind of tapes?"

"I had my recorder on most of the day. I don't think he knew about it." She wondered miserably what ethics were involved in betraying someone to save his life.

"Anything juicy?" Raymond raised a hopeful eyebrow.

"Listen, Dave. If I do this, I said *if*, there are going to be some ground rules, or it's no deal. One – I don't want any direct quoting from the tapes. You can paraphrase or use the material anonymously for in-depth analysis, okay?"

He nodded.

"Two – I retain the right to edit and censor personal material not related directly to the convoy or the issues involved here."

Now it was Raymond's turn to hesitate. Finally he stuck out his hand and said, "It's a deal. Where's the stuff."

"It's in the cab of the truck. I'll be back in five minutes."

As she started away, he took her arm. "Melissa, this is really a good thing you're doing, the best thing for everybody."

"That's what I keep telling myself. But why do I feel so lousy?"

They exchanged wan smiles that acknowledged they both knew the answer to that one but would rather not think about it, and he let her go. He watched her out of sight in the crowd that had gathered around the three catering trucks that had made a special run from town and were doing a land-office business.

"She's got guts," he mused aloud to no one in particular. "They don't make many like that anymore. Probably never did."

Meanwhile, the Duck was shifting his feet nervously, listening for his cue from the preacher and wondering just what in hell he was doing here. He knew, of course, how he'd gotten here, but that was a different story.

He had been traveling around the camp from contest to contest and group to group, trying to do what he could, which wasn't much, to keep the park more or less in one piece until the Governor arrived. Suddenly he felt a hand tugging at his sleeve and turned around to find the Widow Woman standing behind him. Just looking at her, he could see that something was up. She didn't look at him when she spoke, and she kept knotting – unknotting her fingers like a young girl.

"Duck, I got to ask you a favor," she blurted out all in a rush.

"Why sure thing, Widow Woman. Anything short of becoming husband number five, that is. I'm a mite too busy for that right now."

She smiled, but she didn't laugh. "Well, that's just it, Duck," she answered shyly. "I got me a number five already. His handle's Badger Bob. Been driving relief for Pocono Pete outta Fresno. Maybe you know him?"

The Duck thought a minute and shook his head. "Only Badger Bob I know used to drive short haul in Texas years ago."

"My Badger Bob's a different one. He's a good man, Duck, and he's a trucker, born and bred. The way we seen it, we been needin each other for a long time now. And at our age, you ain't got a lotta time for courtin. So we went to see that preacher man that's been travelin with the convoy, and he's willin to perform the ceremony anytime we want, for free, in honor of the occasion and all."

The Duck took a step and gave her a big enough hug to squeeze the breath from her body. "That's mighty fine, Widow Woman," he said, meaning it. "It appears to me that you got everything under control."

"Well, there's one thing, I ain't got, ain't ever had actually." She hesitated and then went on. "I don't know if I ever told you, but my father was a drinkin man. He just drunk himself plumb out of existence by the time I was twelve years old."

She paused for a gulp of air and continued. "First time I was married, we eloped on a run to Vegas. Wasn't nobody to care anyways. Since then, every time I got married, I been given myself away and skippin over that part of the ceremony when we come to it. Well, this time is the last, I can feel it in my bones, and I kinda wanted somebody to do that for me, just once, and I was wonderin if you're not too . . ."

"Widow Woman, I'd be more than proud to stand up for you."

She gave him a huge smile of relief. She wasn't a woman that was used to asking favors. "Nothin to it really. You just walk up to the preacher with me and when he says, 'who gives this woman to be married?', you just say 'I do.' "

Then her expression changed and she went back to being the shy, young girl again. "By the way, just so's you'll know," she said, studying her hands, "I got me a new handle, now that I ain't a widow woman anymore. Me'n Bob sort of decided it on the way in."

"Why, sure enough. Makes sense to me. What's it gonna be."

Now she was really blushing. All he could see were her cheeks and the top of her head. When she raised her eyes, they were almost angry, and be damned to him if he laughed. "Tonalove," she said defiantly.

"I said 'who gives this here woman to enter into holy wedlock with this here man?'" The Reverend Joshua Duncan Sloane's voice broke into the Duck's flashback impatiently.

"I do," he responded with some confusion.

Satisfied, the Reverend turned his attention back to the bridal couple.

"Do you, Ah Tonalove, take this man here for your lawful wedded husband, to have and . . ."

"A big ten-four on that," the Widow Woman interrupted. "You can skip the rest of that stuff. By this time, I know it by heart." Now that she was actually into the ceremony, she was as comfortable as a fish in water.

"I do," said Badger Bob before the Reverend had a chance to even begin the question.

"Well," he said not in the least put off, "I now pronounce you man and wife." He motioned the two of them together for the kiss. "God bless you," he intoned, "and keep the hammer down."

The crowd, who had been listening to the ceremony over the public address auxiliary of the Reverend's CB, broke into a huge cheer. After he'd taken his turn at kissing the bride, the Duck moved on, looking for Melissa. He didn't know for sure why, but he wanted to see her.

A half hour later, he was still searching. As he passed by a line of bushes shielding a picnic table, he heard something that stopped him dead in his tracks. It was his own voice!

"End of the line for us, too, I reckon," it said.

He charged around the hedge to find Melissa and Dave Raymond sitting on opposite sides of the table with the tape recorder between them. Raymond had a pad in front of him and was taking notes.

Melissa saw him coming and switched off the machine. Maybe he hadn't heard, although from the look on his face, she'd have to say that wasn't likely. Well, nothing ventured ...

"Congratulations. You're a celebrity. I just sold you to the networks," she said brightly as if it were the most natural thing in the world. Raymond just sat there trying to get his jaw to stay closed. The Duck walked up between them and leaned forward on the table. His expression made the approach of the sandstorm seem mild by comparison.

"You mean you sold me out."

"It's the only way," Melissa tried to explain. "You can beat any part of this with good publicity, and we can get it for you."

"That's absolutely right," Raymond put in.

The Duck turned to him as if he'd just noticed a mosquito in his ear. "This is between her'n me. If I want any shit out of you, I'll knock it out. Why don't you just take your little pad and git."

Raymond got. He had his notes anyway. It was going to be quite a story. When they were alone, the Duck turned back to Melissa.

"You know, you're a very slick lady," he said bitterly. "You really are. You find yourself a little old convoy – why not make it a protest march? Then it's news. And then you get this old boy who's drivin front door to shoot his mouth off to a television camera, and then you collect – a lot – right?"

Melissa was stung all the way through, as much by the contempt in his voice as his words.

"Big Man," she snapped back. "You can't take it. Is that it? Don't lay all of this on me Duck. You started this convoy. Nobody else. And it got too big for you. It took you out of your safe little truck, your safe little life."

"Well, if that's it, how about gettin *out* of my safe little truck *and* my safe little life right now. How far were you fixing to take this? Exclusive story – the sex life of a trucker? All you had to do was ask, I'd've told you."

"No need to ask. I've already seen part of your collection."

They stood there for a moment toe to toe, betrayed, ready but unwilling to strike at each other. Suddenly a new voice entered the conversation. It was Big Nasty, who came puffing up accompanied by a couple of other truckers.

"Hey, Duck," he called. "You better get your ass in gear. The Governor's here."

As if summoned up by Big Nasty's announcement, a luxurious Apollo Motorhome with police escort front and rear and followed by a string of media cars pulled up on the access road a few yards away. The Duck looked at Melissa for a parting shot.

"I want your shit out of my cab and out of my life, hear?"

She gathered up the tape recorder and started heading back toward the truck. "With pleasure," she sneered over her shoulder. "There's no telling what I might catch in that sleeper of yours."

One of the police escort hopped off his bike and opened the Motorhome door. From it stepped the Governor followed by Arnoldi and Meyers. After a brief consultation with Arnoldi, the Governor walked over to the Duck until both men were bathed in the lightning of exploding flashbulbs. He held out his hand and said, "Rubber Duck? Glad to meet you."

The Duck shook the offered hand and was immediately annoyed when the Governor wouldn't let go until the flashbulbs subsided.

"This is Senator Meyers," the Governor said indicating Big Hank, "and I gather you and my aide, Chuck Arnoldi, have already met." The Duck and Arnoldi exchanged a look that would have killed any man foolish enough to get in the way of it.

The Governor rubbed his hands together and continued. "This is some gathering you have here, Rubber Duck. You're quite a leader."

"I didn't set out to lead anybody, it just happened," the Duck answered honestly.

"Still you've brought some well-deserved attention to some important issues here," the Governor went on, his focus going right over the Duck's shoulder to the cameras beyond.

"There's a growing disenchantment in this country, and not only with the fifty-five mile an hour speed limit. It seems to me that's what we're touching on here. I believe it's about time that those of us in public office listened to the voice of the people."

"No shit."

The Governor's poise didn't even waver. "So why don't you step into my office," he suggested, pointing to the Motorhome with an even wider smile, "and we'll talk."

"Why? The people can talk for themselves."

The Governor looked around the three and four deep circle of truckers that had gathered. "I'm sure they can," he agreed, "but I'm not so sure I could understand them if they all started talking at once. I am sure these men will accept you as their spokesman. Won't you boys?"

"You bet your ass we will," a voice from beyond the lights answered.

"Give em hell, Duck," another called out from the opposite side of the circle. There was general chorus of yeah's and stick-it-to-em's. When it died down, the Governor turned back to the Duck.

"You see?" he said. "You underestimate yourself." He indicated the door to the Motorhome with an outstretched arm.

"Maybe I do," the Duck allowed, reluctantly moving toward it, "but that don't mean I'm likely to overestimate anybody else, includin you."

The Governor gave him a thoughtful glance. "You know," he half-offered, half-observed, "this could turn out to be one hell of an interesting night for us both."

CHAPTER TEN

Spider Mike was happy. In another couple of hours he'd be home. By now even, he might be a father. A father! He rolled the word around in his mouth, trying to get a good grip on it. His own father had been killed in a railroad accident when Mike was five years old and his mother had never remarried. Mike had left home for the Marines as soon as he had been old enough to convince his mother to sign the papers. A year as a supply driver in Vietnam had cured him of the military for good.

He had met Carol at a friend's party shortly after he returned home, and for both of them that had been it. She had stayed on her job in the accounting section of the bank, and he had driven long-haul at Beacons until they got enough money together for the down payment on the truck. After that it seemed no time at all before she told him she was pregnant.

At first, he didn't want her to be. Sure, they were planning on having kids someday, but it was too damn soon. They needed more of a life together first, a chance to get set up with a little money ahead instead of the staggering amount owed when he allowed himself to think about it. Then one night when he was lying awake after Carol had fallen asleep beside him and trying to figure how in hell they could possibly handle another mouth to feed, not to mention clothes, doctors and all that, it suddenly struck him like a good right cross to the stomach.

Whether he liked it or not, whether there was any way to deal with it or not, he was going to be a father, not just a husband and lover but the head of a family. He became acutely aware of how much he had missed having his own father around when he had been growing up. He and his mother had been close, since there had been no other children to divide their attention, but they had never been willing or able to create a sense of family, of a self-contained unit living with and for themselves within the wider circles of relatives and friends. Now he was going to be part of a family, his own, and he was going to bust his ass to see that it would be the very best family possible, no matter what it took.

His mind completely blown, he had waked Carol up to tell her what had happened to him. They had both cried a little at the pure joy of it all, and then they had made love again just to celebrate. And now, it was happening – his child was on the way to being born. "Hang on, honey," he called aloud to Carol over the dwindling miles that still separated them. "I'm coming."

He stretched and rotated his neck to get out some of the stiffness that had built up since he had left the convoy. He didn't mind admitting that in spite of his parting words to the Duck, he had been pretty uptight about lighting out on his own. The first few miles had been torture, right on the edge of Panicsville. If he had gotten busted even overnight, he would have been too late, and somehow he knew deep inside him where there weren't any words or even thoughts, that he had to be there when his new life, all of their new lives began.

Now that he was over the Texas border, he felt a little less like he was walking on eggs. For one thing, he was far enough from the convoy now to claim that he'd never heard of it in case he got stopped. He felt a twinge of guilt at that thought, after all if the Duck hadn't pitched in to help him out, there probably wouldn't have been a convoy to begin with. But he told himself that his getting busted wasn't going to help the others out any, and besides he knew they'd want him to make it back any way he had to. They were that kind of men, and he'd do the same for them someday if it ever came to that.

He had to keep reminding himself to keep his speed legal no matter how much of a hurry he was in. With only a couple of bucks in his pocket, a speeding ticket could be as deadly as armed robbery, considering the schedule he was on. He passed the ALVAREZ TEXAS sign and slowed to five miles an hour below the posted thirty-five limit. The highway was deserted as you would expect at this time on a Sunday night, but this was dangerous territory, the Texas equivalent of the stretch of I-40 back in Arizona that belonged to Lyle. The truckers that drove this route regularly had a name for Alvarez – Trucker's Hell – and they all swore that Tiny Alvarez, the cop that ran the town, was as close to the devil as you'd ever want to come in this life. Mike personally had never had any trouble the few times he'd come this way, but you couldn't prove anything by that.

Just then he heard the blast of a siren. His side mirror was completely filled by the flashing lights of the bubble gum machine right on his tail. The bastards must have snuck out from a side road somewhere. He checked his speed – still thirty so he was okay there. Maybe it was just a taillight gone, or they might just feel like hassling for no good reason. He'd heard about one driver who'd gotten busted in Montana for having one white in his glove compartment. But even there he was okay. He'd taken a couple and thrown out the rest of his speed right after he left the convoy.

Behind him the siren sounded again, and the cruiser accelerated to cut him off in front. Resisting the impulse to put the hammer down and drive right over the sons of bitches, Mike pulled over to the side. At least he was clean, he knew that. Even in Alvarez they couldn't bust you for nothing.

The cop that got out of the patrol car to meet him looked more like a bear than a man. He stood close to six foot-five and with that southern sheriff belly of his must have gone about two-seventy, two-seventy-five. Backlighted by the flashing red lights of his car, he appeared even bigger. Mike had heard about him – it was Tiny Alvarez, himself.

"A little hard of hearin aren't you, boy?" Tiny opened up when they'd met about halfway between the two vehicles.

"I heard you, but I thought you musta been after somebody else since I was doing at least five miles under the limit," Mike answered, figuring he could afford to be nice since he for sure had the truth on his side.

Tiny took a long, pointed look up and down the deserted highway before he said, "I don't see anybody else around, do you, boy?"

"No, I guess not," Mike admitted.

"You guess not? You know damn good and well not. Now why don't you just hand over that log book and make it easy on us both."

Mike passed it over. He couldn't figure out what this was all about, but it couldn't be speeding or anything else he could see.

Tiny took his time checking out the book under the truck headlights. "Michael Golden," he read slowly. "You the one they call Spider Mike?"

"Some of the time." Mike's stomach started to tighten up on him. There was definitely something wrong here. He'd have to really watch his ass.

Just then a car that looked and sounded like the loser in a demolition derby rounded the curve on two wheels and squealed to a stop inches from the tailgate of the truck. When the driver climbed out, Mike knew. He didn't believe it, but he knew.

"Lyle." Mike's mind was still reeling. This all seemed more like a nightmare than any kind of reality. "This isn't your town."

"It ain't my state either," Lyle replied comfortably, "but that don't make any difference. You got a string of warrants on you stretchin all the way to Arizona." He pointed to Tiny. "You know who this here is?"

"Yeah, it's Tiny Alvarez." Mike figured he might as well lay it on the line. The time when playing dumb would get him anywhere was long past.

"Call him Your Honor," Lyle suggested. "He's the justice of the peace here, too."

"Yeah," Tiny rumbled in a voice as big as his chest. "We figured you'd be passin through here so I been waitin up for ya. Wouldn't of known a thing about it though, if it hadn't been for my special deputy here." He took a badge from his pocket and handed it to Lyle.

"Tiny don't like truckers, son," Lyle said as he tucked the badge away in his shirt pocket. "Not at all."

"Yeah, me'n Lyle got something in common," Tiny said with a blubbery chuckle.

Suddenly he pulled Mike's arms behind his back and

snapped on the cuffs all in one motion. For Mike, it was like being grabbed by a tornado.

"Hey, don't do this now," he protested. "I got to get to the hospital over in Fort Plains. My wife is in labor." Now that the prisoner was secured, both of the men ignored him and went on talking to each other.

"Tell me something, Tiny. How do you people over here deal with an assault against an officer charge?" Lyle wanted to know.

Tiny shook his head. "We don't deal with it," he answered. "What we deal with is an escape charge. Like for instance I'm gonna turn my back right now, and whattaya wanta bet that boy tries to escape."

He turned around deliberately and stood staring out across the highway. For just a split second, Mike thought about trying it, but he knew he couldn't get ten yards with his arms cuffed behind his back like they were. The bastards had him good – no use giving them a chance to shoot him on top of it. He stood his ground, waiting.

"Yup, you're right," Lyle said after a while, moving closer. "He's damn sure tryin to escape."

"Then you better quick do somethin about it," Tiny suggested.

Lyle did something about it. First he brought his knee straight up into Mike's groin, doubling him over with the pain. He followed that up with a karate chop to the back of the neck. Then he yanked Mike's body up from the pavement by its handcuffed wrists and propped him up against the truck.

"I been through a lot for this," he grunted as he planted a solid right cross on the trucker's defenseless cheekbone. "And I plan to make it worth my while."

A couple of minutes later when Mike's face was a solid mass of blood from the broken nose and missing teeth, Tiny pulled Lyle off. "T'ain't fair you hoggin all the fun," he objected. "You got to save a little for me, now."

He positioned himself solidly in front of the drooping body and smashed a thunderous right into the solar plexus. Mike's legs went out from under him and dropped him to the street.

"Looks like he ain't gonna try no more escapes tonight," Tiny observed with satisfaction. "If you'll help me load his carcass into your car, we'll take him in."

"Why my car?" Lyle asked, puzzled.

"Just got the blood cleaned offa my seats last week, and it don't come cheap I can tell you," Tiny explained. "That vehicle of yourn looks prit near ready for the junkyard anyhow."

Spider Mike woke up to a broom handle being poked gently against his shoulder, one of the few spots on his body that seemed not to have been permanently destroyed. He opened the one eye that would open at all and got a fuzzy view of an old black man in work clothes and a Peterbilt Truck cap. He was Moses J. Malone, part-time janitor at the Alvarez city jail. Moses had watched a string of Tiny's victims pass through the jail but this boy was in the worst shape he'd seen yet.

"Kid," he called softly when he saw the eyelid flicker, "are you all right?"

Mike could only groan. His tongue had swelled up to at least half the size of his mouth.

"I heard them talking," Moses whispered. "You from the convoy?"

This time Mike managed to croak out a yes and nod his head.

"Don't worry, kid. I'll get help," the old man promised. "Just take it easy."

After propping his broom against the wall, Moses tiptoed into the squad room. It was empty. The voices of Lyle and Tiny filtered through the door from the front steps where they'd moved to escape the heat.

"I tell you, Tiny, it's a cinch," Lyle was complaining. "And then we got the big cheese, none of this chicken feed."

"What makes you think he'd come alone?"

"Because I know the Duck. He ain't the kind of man to drag anybody else in on this, especially when they got amnesty, which you an I know they're surer'n shit gonna git. It's a snap, I tell you . . ."

"No, I ain't gonna risk it," Tiny decided.

"You ain't just the least bit chicken shit, are you there, old buddy?"

"Now you listen here, Wallace. You want to risk turnin that buncha sonsabitches loose on your town in Arizona, you go right ahead. You ain't properly deputized over here if it comes to that."

"Sure, Tiny. Sure. Don't you go gettin riled at me. I'd just like ta get my hands on a few more of them gearjammers. That's all."

"One's enough," Tiny opined. "We'll give him a couple of days to recover, then we and him can have another go round if you're in the mood."

Moses flicked on the CB switch and spoke very softly. "Break one-nine, Break one-nine. Emergency ten-thirty-three. Any westbound eighteen-wheeler read me? Come on."

A few miles out of Alvarez to the west, the Silver Streak was haulin ass for Clovis where he hoped to unload in record time and make it up to Tucumcari before the party was over. "I got a copy on you," he answered. "Go."

"I need a message relayed west to the Rubber Duck and the convoy. Spider Mike is in jail in Alvarez, Texas. Lyle Wallace and Tiny Alvarez beat him near to death. He needs help. You understand that?"

"Ten-four good buddy. I read you good. I'll relay it on up."

Moses switched off the CB with relief. Now it was up to them, but if he knew his truckers, and he did, that message would hit the convoy in a matter of minutes. He shook his fist at the door behind which Lyle and Tiny were still chewing the fat.

"The day of reckonin comin," he chortled. "In fact, it jus done *arrived*."

The conference had gone better than anybody expected right from the start. After they had pushed their way through the reporters into the livingroom of the motorhome, the Governor had offered drinks around. Big Hank and Arnoldi headed for the bar and began mixing themselves up something tall with a splash of water.

"What do you say, Duck?" the Governor urged again.

"Thanks but no thanks. I'm runnin on speed right now. The booze'll only bring me down."

"As you wish." The Governor waved him to a chair and took a seat opposite on the couch. The Duck noticed that he wasn't drinking either.

"Now as I was saying out there, you've called attention to some very important issues with the convoy of yours – where are you going?"

In the middle of the sentence, the Duck had stood up and headed for the door. He paused with his hand on the knob. "If that's the kind of bullshit you're figurin on feedin me, I'm gonna get out of here while there's still room to breathe."

"See? I told you it was a mistake coming down here," Meyer cut in from the car. "The only way to deal with rabble like that is a good knock on the head. That's all they understand."

"Shut up, Henry," the Governor said quietly as the Duck turned to go. He walked over to the door and faced the Duck head on. "So you think that what I've been saying is bullshit," he challenged.

The Duck nodded. "It sure ain't nothin else."

"Well, you're right. But so what?" There was an audible gasp from one of the two aides. "It's nothing you don't do yourself from time to time, I'll bet. Tell me you don't get on that CB radio of yours and ham it up whenever you get the chance."

The Duck smiled ruefully. His grip on the doorknob loosened.

"The point is that we've got a problem here," the Governor went on seriously. "And we also have an opportunity to do something about it if we work together. What do you say?"

He put out his hand. After a moment, the Duck took a step back from the door and shook it. "Sounds fair to me," he conceded. He gave Big Hank and Arnoldi a hard look. "However, there's only one of me here," he said pointedly.

The Governor got the message. "Henry and Chuck, when you finish those drinks why don't you two go outside and entertain our friends from the press," he suggested.

When they had gone, he motioned the Duck back to his original seat and poured himself a drink.

"Okay," he said, "tell me. What is it that you people really want?"

"I can't speak for everybody, but for me it's a say in how I do my work and live my life, providin I ain't hurtin anybody else," the Duck answered after a moment of thought.

"That sounds reasonable. In fact the U.S. Constitution is supposed to guarantee it. How about some specifics we can work with here and now?"

Suddenly the door flew open and Arnoldi stuck his head inside. "Would it be safe to tell the media that the talks are making progress?" he asked importantly.

"It might be if you shut that door and kept your nose out of here." the Governor answered sharply. "Don't come in again unless I send for you. And that goes for Henry, too," he added for the benefit of the shadow lurking behind Arnoldi in the doorway.

When quiet had settled in, he turned back to the Duck. "You were going to say?"

"What I was goin to say was about that fifty-five mile an hour limit. I'll tell you something maybe you don't know. Them big rigs like mine are built for long hauls at sixty-five, seventy-five, not fifty-five. They're more economical at higher speeds."

The Governor took a pull of his drink and looked skeptical.

"You don't believe me?" the Duck went on. "It's been scientifically proven. They sent two trucks across country. Same make trucks. Same weight load, only one of them drove fast and the other obeyed all the laws. Guess which one got the best mileage? The one going faster. It's true."

"So you get what? An extra half mile to the gallon or something like that?" The Governor had sat up on the edge of the couch. He was interested but still a long way from being convinced.

"Somethin like that. And I'll tell you what else you get. Say I drive fifteen hours a day, right?"

"Right." Despite his native political caution, the Governor felt himself being sucked in. 'It's a pity this guy didn't go into politics,' he thought. 'Give him a couple of years to learn the ropes, and he'd drive people like Arnoldi right out of the arena, which wouldn't be such a bad idea at that.'

"Okay," the Duck went on. "Before the damn politicians changed the law, I was makin something like sixty-five miles an hour average. Now, say I go ten less miles each hour I work, which is one hundred and fifty less miles a day. You know what that is?"

The Governor shook his head helplessly.

"A fifteen percent cut in my pay. How'd you like the government to just up some day and cut your salary fifteen percent without you gettin in an if, or an and, or a maybe? I obey the law the way it is now, I'd be broke like that."

"I'll be damned." The Governor was convinced. "I can see where you certainly have a point."

"Damn right I got a point," the Duck rushed on, getting it all out. "And I'll tell you something else, too. Those snake politicians and those damn oil companies are all playing kissey-face. The bastards got nothin better to do than bury their gold and think about new and different ways of screwing Mr. and Mrs. You and Me."

"Easy there, friend," the Governor protested. "You're talking to one of those 'snake politicians', you know. Still, I can understand what you're saying, and I've got a pretty good idea that most of those people outside would agree with you. The problem now is how to do something about it without having to put all of you behind bars for the next ten years."

Within a half-hour, they had hammered out a feasible program. Arnoldi was called in as a secretary to put the major points in writing.

"Let's see here," he said, studying his notes. "What we seem to have is an agreement to hold a state referendum in the fall, including a special section to deal with interstate trucking. The State Department of Transportation will begin immediate testing of diesel fuel consumption at various rates of speed with the results to be forwarded to each of the state congressmen and also made available to the public before the referendum takes place. Finally a general amnesty is to be declared for all members of the convoy, and it is to cover specifically all offenses committed within the state. And we will do all in our power to persuade Governor Jordan of Arizona to follow a similar course."

The look on his face was sufficient testimony to what he thought of the whole damn thing. The only consolation was that old Meyers was really going to blow his top on this one. There was a commotion outside. Suddenly the trailer door was thrown open by the Widow Woman with such force that it bounced off the wall.

"Duck," she cried out, ignoring the other two men, "they got Mike. I just got a relay message on the CB. Lyle and Tiny Alvarez are holdin him over in Alvarez, Texas. They said they beat him half to death, real bad."

The Duck turned to the Governor. "Will you help us?" he asked, putting it all on the line.

"I'll do what I can," the Governor promised," but officially I have no power there." He checked his watch. "Perhaps by tomorrow . . . What are you doing?"

The Duck had gotten up and was headed toward the door. "We're goin to wipe that shithole off the map," the Widow Woman answered for him.

"But wait. There are things we can accomplish here," the Governor protested. Arnoldi was standing with his mouth agape. Could it be that politics wasn't the soft touch he'd figured when he graduated from the University?

The Widow Woman paused in the doorway like an ancient spirit of vengeance framed against the turmoil outside. "It's too late," she said.

The Duck fought his way through the hands and voices clutching at him to the Reverend Sloane's van. After a short conference with the Reverend, he climbed on the van's top and used the P.A. to address the crowd, which by now included practically everybody in the camp.

"Quiet down a minute and let me say my piece," he ordered. When the chaos had subsided to a rumble, he went on. "I guess you all heard about Spider Mike over in Truckers Hell."

"You're damn right we did,' shouted an angry voice from

the back. The Duck simply looked in its direction until there was silence again.

"The Governor can't do anything at least until morning cause it ain't his state. So I'm going. The rest of you scatter. It's over." He raised a hand to check the rising reaction from the crowd. "This is between Lyle and me, and you've all got amnesty, so keep out of it . . . split . . . better not stick too many of you together. Catch you on the flip-flop."

He jumped down from the van and pushed his way through the stunned group toward his truck. At the edge of the crowd, Dave Raymond fell in step with him.

"There's something you ought to know about those tapes tonight."

"Is there?" The Duck's voice was indifferent. He wasn't about to open up that mess again.

"Yes. I blackmailed Melissa into letting me hear them by threatening to destroy you in the media if she didn't. She only did it to save your neck." By now Raymond was practically running to keep up with the Duck's longer stride.

They reached the truck and the Duck jumped up into the cab. He took a quick look over the crowd, but Melissa was nowhere to be seen. But what difference did it make? What could he say anyway? He looked down to the reporter standing by the door.

"Thanks," he said, "but it don't really matter now."

He started the engine and began threading his way through the small groups of truckers that had gathered together to talk. Once he was clear, he gunned it and roared out of the park headed east.

Pig Pen was laying back oblivious of all that was going, and pretty nearly everything else. On one side of him in his sleeper lay Linda on the other was an equally worn out Arliss. Both girls were asleep with their heads nestled on his shoulders. He allowed himself an even wider smile. They sure didn't make these young ones the way they used to. Course maybe there was something to what that woman had told him in a bar back in El Paso years ago about how some certain people improved with age like wine. Right at this particular moment, he didn't really care.

When he heard the tapping on his cab window, he didn't believe it, didn't want to believe it. He closed his eyes and pretended not to hear. But it went on louder and louder, eventually accompanied by a female voice calling his name. Son of a bitch! He slid his arms out from under the girls' heads, pulled on his pants, and crawled out into the cab.

For a moment, his mind refused to take in what his eyes were telling him. The campground was practically deserted. And Melissa was standing there beside his cab with a suitcase on either side of her. He rolled down the window and asked, "What happened? Where's everybody? Where's the Duck?" in a thoroughly bewildered voice.

"They've gone," she answered. "Spider Mike was beaten and thrown in jail by Lyle and somebody named Tiny Alvarez. The Duck's gone to help him."

"By himself? Where's everybody else?"

She nodded. "He wanted it that way. The Governor declared an amnesty. The Duck told them to scatter after he left, and they did."

"You mean he's goin into Truckers Hell by hisself to try and spring Mike?"

Melissa nodded again. Pig Pen groped back in the sleeper for his boots. "Well, he ain't," he declared, beginning to pull them on.

Melissa stepped up on the running board and looked straight in at him. "Take me with you," she said.

"Well, I don't know about that," Pig Pen hedged. "How come you didn't go with the Duck?"

"We had a fight," she answered truthfully. "He threw me out."

"Well, there you see, if he don't want you along, then I ain't got no call to . . ."

"Pig Pen," she interrupted, "I love him."

He could see by her eyes that it was true. He cast one last longing glance at the sleeper. Well, them girls wouldn't be nothing but extra weight anyways if it came to a fight, which he could pretty well figure it would. He allowed himself a few farewell squeezes before waking them with a couple of slaps on the butt.

"Come on, girls," he said regretfully. "You got to hit the road. I got business."

"What kind of business?" Arliss wanted to know.

"Nothin that concerns either one of you. Now you got to go. I'm in a mighty big rush."

"Hold your horses," Linda complained. "What's gonna happen to us?"

Pig Pen took a look out the window. A bunch of the younger truckers had stayed behind to finish out a slalom driveoff.

"I got the feelin you girls is gonna do fine, just fine," he answered grinding his teeth at the waste of it all.

When they were out on the highway and headed east, Melissa suggested, "Why don't you use the radio and see if anyone else is around? We could probably use all the help we can get."

She was right. Pig Pen reached for the mike. "Break one-nine. This here's the Love Machine headin east. Anybody out there got a copy on me? Come on."

"Widow Woman, ah . . . Tonalove, here. Got you. What's your twenty?"

"Just left the park. Don't see no markers yet. Where you headed."

"Same place you are, I expect. Me'n Badger Bob talked it over, an we ain't about to let the Duck go into that hellhole all by hisself."

"Anybody else out there?" Pig Pen called.

"You got me, Big Nasty," a voice replied. "Sounds like fun to me. I ain't about to miss this for nothin. Anybody else? Come on."

"Count the Bald Eagle in," a new voice came on. "I done some time in that shithole years ago, and I ain't likely to ever forget it."

"Me too," a new voice said. "This here's Mexican Pete, and Tiny Alvarez busted my brother three years ago. He ain't drove since."

"You got Dusty Dan here," a final voice answered. "I get the chance I'll drump this load a lumber right on toppa that fuckin jail."

"Okey, dokey," Pig Pen came on when there was no more responses," we all better git the hammer down and keep her there. We got a mighty good man out there in our front door, and we'd best be haulin ass ifn we expect to close it up on him by the time get to Alvarez."

"You ought to know all about smells with them go-go girls of yourn," Big Nasty snickered.

"You just shut your face about that," Pig Pen sputtered. "Save it for Tiny and Lyle. This ain't exactly no picnic were goin to, ya know."

CHAPTER ELEVEN

The Duck pulled up on the rise overlooking Alvarez, Texas and slumped over the wheel, staring out at the little town. Pretty soon it would be full dawn. He hadn't slept for over twenty-four hours now and he could feel it in every bone in his body. He dropped another white and waited for the rush to come on. He didn't know for sure what he intended to do. He figured he'd just haul ass up to the jail and try to take them by surprise. After that he'd do whatever he had to. Sometimes it didn't pay to think too far ahead.

He felt the sudden surge of energy from the speed just at the time he caught the distant sound of the engines behind him. Before he had time to figure out what was going on, they'd pulled up three on a side with the Widow Woman next to him on the left and Pig Pen on the right.

"You didn't think we'd let you get away with this all by yourself," the Widow Woman's voice came over the CB.

"Yeah," Pig Pen put on. "You can't expect a man to be satisfied with just one piece of ole Lyle's ass. It was mighty tasty as I recall."

Each of the drivers sat erect in his seat, staring straight ahead. On Pig Pen's advice, Melissa had crawled out of view back in the sleeper so as not to create a distraction at a critical time. The Duck's indecision was gone. Now he knew damn well what they were going to do. He let out a war-whoop and put the pedal to the metal. As one, the seven trucks charged, four and three abreast, towards the sleeping town.

Tiny and Lyle had spent the night playing poker at the jail and were still at it. Not that they weren't tired, but they had started on a bottle and got to talking about this bust and that, and before they knew it, it was dawn.

Suddenly Lyle became aware of a distant rumble that the

morning sunshine outside told him couldn't be thunder. "What's that?" he asked looking up from his pair of threes that would probably take the pot.

"What?" Tiny answered irritably, not even glancing up from his cards. As usual for the last couple of hours, he was looking at a jack-high nothing and had the feeling he was about to lose his ass again.

"Listen," Lyle commanded.

The rumble had turned into a rapidly approaching roar. Tiny jumped up and headed to the door for a look-see with Lyle right on his heels. He burst out into the street and took a look in the direction of the sound, which had gotten even louder now that there was no building to muffle it.

"Holy shit," he breathed.

What they saw were seven big rig diesels in two rows four and three wide tearassing down the highway into town at a good seventy, seventy-five miles an hour. Tiny ran back into the office, grabbed a shotgun and hustled Lyle into the black-and-white parked in front. With Lyle driving, they pulled down the street a couple of blocks in the direction of the approaching trucks. Escape lay at the Interstate onramp at Eighth Street, if they could make it. The charging convoy poured it on, and it became apparent that the cruiser was trapped. Confused, Lyle pulled over and watched them come.

When the first wave hit the outskirts of town where the highway narrowed from four lanes to two, they put the hammer down even harder and maintained perfect formation. The two outside trucks ran their outer wheels up on the sidewalk and just kept barreling straight ahead. Parking meters were flattened or bent like jackstraws in a blowdown. The newsrack in front of the hotel went flying in an explosion of papers, metal, and wood. A motorcycle parked at the curb in clear violation of the town ordinance against all night parking went spinning up on the sidewalk and through the hardware store window.

After watching a couple of blocks of this, Tiny jabbed Lyle out of his paralysis. "Let's get the hell out of here," he screamed." Head for the station."

Lyle spun a quick U, right into a Buick, which was trying

to get the hell out of there itself. The two cars locked bumpers, immobilizing them both. Precious seconds were wasted trying to back the vehicles off. Suddenly, Tiny threw open his door. "Run for it," he yelled. "It's the only chance."

He sprinted across the street toward the comparative safety of the back door of the bank. But there was only room for one in the doorway, and Lyle stood terrified in the middle of the street a little too long. When the lead trucks were almost upon him, he made a desperate try for the safety of the public park across the street.

But he had been marked. Flanked by the Widow Woman and Pig Pen, the Duck roared up over the curb and into the park itself barely yards behind the fleeing man. Maintaining their unbroken line and effectively cutting off any escape to the side, the three big rigs cut a swath through the park in pursuit. Benches were smashed flat, small trees were ripped from the ground or bent under. Pig Pen drove straight through a drinking fountain, leaving a ten foot gusher in his wake.

Lyle tried taking refuge behind the chain link backstop of the baseball field, but the three trucks drove right through it uprooting poles and dropping tattered strings of fencing over their cabs and trailers like metal lace. Then he darted into a narrow alley between two sheet metal gardener's shacks. The trucks simply came straight on, stewing the grass with tools, equipment and jagged sheets of tin.

Lyle screamed then, although he could hardly hear himself above the roaring engines, and made a last desperate dash across the street into the station. He closed the door, panting, and staggered over to the gun rack on the opposite wall. He had just managed to break loose a shotgun when the whole front of the building caved in, scattering desks, chairs, filing cabinets, and pinning him to the wall behind the debris. The gun fell clattering from his hands into the middle of the floor beyond his reach.

The Duck stepped out of his rig slow and easy, brushing some dust from his pants, and walked through what was left of the wall.

"Where's Mike?" he demanded.

Lyle jabbed a finger toward the rear of the building.

"Back there in his cell," he answered flatly. The Widow Woman and Pig Pen, who had come in right behind their leader, grabbed up the keys and rushed through the door into the cell block.

Taking advantage of the diversion Lyle tried edging toward the gun on the floor, but the Duck was too quick for him. He walked over, picked up the weapon and pumped a shell into the chamber.

"Don't make me do it, Lyle," he warned. "I want to too much."

There was a scrabbling, dragging sound as Pig Pen and the Widow Woman appeared supporting Spider Mike between them. His face was one huge purple bruise caked over with blood, and one of his legs didn't appear to be functioning all that well.

"Yeah, and I feel it, too," he said quietly in answer to the Duck's look of disbelief.

The Duck pointed to Lyle with the barrel of the gun. "Well, it's your turn now," he said grimly. "Work him over."

In the stark silence of the room, Mike hobbled over to Lyle. He stooped very slowly and picked up a broken rung from one of the chairs. He raised it high above the head of the flinching man and then slowly let it drop.

"I got better things to do," he said painfully through his swollen lips and missing teeth. "I got a wife and child to get back to."

The Duck set the shotgun carefully against the wall. "Well, I don't," he said, rolling up his sleeves. "Come on, Lyle. You and me's gonna meet outside. This is one time you ain't gonna hide behind your monkey suit."

Lyle followed him out into the street for the fight they'd both been waiting for, probably since the day they were born. It was not a long battle, but it made up in viciousness what it lacked in length.

First the Duck knocked him sprawling with a solid right cross. Then Lyle came back with a savage butt to the stomach that sent the Duck reeling to the ground himself. Rolling rapidly to one side and then the other to avoid Lyle's repeated kicks, the Duck finally managed to grab a foot and send the other man spinning to the street.

When they had both regained their feet, the Duck planted a solid one-two in Lyle's breadbasket and then grabbed him from behind in a vise-like bearhug. Slowly, despite Lyle's kicks and squirms, he was lifted off the ground and thrown a good four feet to the pavement where his head cracked solidly but not lethally against the curb. It was over. He was down for good.

There was a chorus of cheers from behind him, and the Duck turned to find Big Nasty, Badger Bob, Mexican Pete, and Dusty Dan standing there holding the unconscious body of Tiny Alvarez at each corner like an grotesque oversized doll. The Bald Eagle brought up the rear carrying the unused riot gun.

"We were trying to help him and he fell down," Big Nasty explained with an appropriately nasty laugh.

"It appears like he weren't the only one," the Bald Eagle observed with a pointed look at the unconscious Lyle.

"Listen, get them two into the cells in there and lock em up good," the Duck ordered." We got to haul our asses out of here, pronto."

When it was all done, they gathered in the street in front of the demolished station. Before he spoke, the Duck looked at each of them, one by one.

"I guess this ends it," he began, his voice low with emotion. "Glad you were here, but now there's really no chance of us stickin together. I do thank you. This time save your own asses, hear." He tried to say more, couldn't, and finally headed for his truck. As if the glue holding them together had suddenly come unstuck, the rest of the group straggled off in the direction of their rigs.

About fifteen miles out of town on a secondary that seemed to be leading nowhere, the Duck pulled over in the shade of a couple of tall trees and shut off the engine. Now that it was over, he could feel how really burnt out he was both mentally and physically. He knew that he had to be planning where to go, what to do next, but his brain seemed to have gone on strike. He became aware of the blood still dripping from his nose and reached back into the sleeper for a rag or something to clean it up with.

Suddenly, amazingly, a clean handkerchief was handed to

him. Before he was able to say a word, Melissa climbed out of the sleeper, took the handkerchief from his hand and began gently wiping the blood from his face.

"What are you doing here?" he demanded as soon as he had convinced himself that she was really there.

She simply shrugged and went on cleaning him up. It was obvious to her, it should be obvious to him, her manner seemed to say. Where else would she be?

"I don't want your head in the same noose I'm wearing," he continued after she had finally finished working on his nose and mouth.

"Well, if you're not going to do it my way, I may as well do it yours." Her tone was that of a woman whose mind is made up. Doubts were for other people.

"I can't have that," the Duck declared firmly, but even as he spoke he realized how much he really wanted it, wanted her somehow to convince him.

Melissa looked at him shrewdly. "Are you a gambler?" she asked suddenly. "I'll bet you are. Otherwise you wouldn't be here, right?"

"This ain't got nothin to do with gambling," he growled. "This whole trip's been a dead sure loser from the word go."

"Ever play liars poker?" she went on, not about to be detoured by that kind of grumbling.

He nodded.

"Have you got two bills?"

He took two ones from his wallet and handed them to her. She moved them around in her hand until they were thoroughly mixed up, then held both out for him to draw. He took the one on his right.

"All right," she said, "make up your hand."

"Before I do that, how about tellin me what we're playing for."

She gave him a direct, mysterious look. "Your way or mine."

"Whatever they may be?"

"Whatever they may be," she acknowledged. "Now make up your hand."

The serial number on the Duck's bill wasn't the worst he'd ever had. He would be able to make three sevens out of it, which was good enough to win most of these games. He sneaked a look at Melissa who was studying her bill with the frowning seriousness of a little child. She glanced over, caught him looking at her, smiled.

"Call," she said.

"Best I can do is three sevens," he said with false humility, ready to claim the win.

She shook her head. "Not good enough," she said. "I've got four fives."

"What? Wait a minute. Let me see that bill." The Duck made a grab, but she pulled it teasingly out of reach.

"Don't you trust me?" she asked in her most untrustworthy voice.

"I guess I'm gonna have to," he conceded, "less'n I want to whup you, too, and take that dollar from you."

She made a fist – it was the first time he had noticed how small and delicate her hands really were – and shook it in his face. "Try it," she challenged. "You know, you've been through a lot in the past twenty-four hours. I'll bet you aren't half as tough as you look."

"All right. You win. What's your way?"

Suddenly, without warning, she was in his arms kissing him gently on the unbruised side of his mouth. After the second kiss, she crawled over on his lap and snuggled her body against him.

"The way I see it, there's only one way now," she whispered softly when they finally came up to catch their breath. She wriggled off his lap and disappeared into the sleeper. "Come on in," she called, laughing, when he just sat there, stunned and unable to get himself together enough to follow her. "I've spent so much time stowing away in here, it's beginning to feel like home."

The voice on the CB radio woke her up. She lay there for a moment, feeling the heavy warmth of the Duck's body next to her, unwilling to move.

"Silver Streak calling Rubber Duck," the voice repeated impatiently. "Are you there? Come on."

Moving carefully so as not to wake him and destroy the first real peace she'd seen on his face since they'd met, Melissa eased herself out of the sleeper and reached for the mike.

"This is the Rubber Duck's truck," she answered. "He's asleep right now."

"Who's this? What's your handle?" the voice demanded.

"This is Mel, uh Dangerous Curves. What do you want?"

"Thank the Lord. We been callin all over the state for the past two hours. Thought maybe the bears'd got ya."

"There's nothing like a bear in sight," Melissa answered. 'Except me,' she thought, giggling and hoping that nobody would drive by while she was sitting there on the seat stark naked.

"Well that's surely the best news of the day," the Silver Streak came back, obviously relieved. "What's your twenty?"

"My what?"

"Your location. Where are ya?"

"We're on some kind of secondary road about twenty miles east of Alvarez. There seems to be a major highway running parallel on a kind of bluff about a quarter of a mile away," she went on, noticing it for the first time.

'Gotcha," a new voice with a Texas twang came in. "You're on old State 54. Know the exact spot. Usedta hunt jackrabbits around there when I was a boy."

"Stay where you are," the Silver Streak advised. "We'll find you. Over and out."

Melissa crawled back into the sleeper, wondering what all that had been about. But there didn't seem to be anything to do about it, so she decided not to waste time worrying. With the kind of situation they were in, an hour was worth at least a week of ordinary life.

Her movements woke up the Duck enough for him to turn and put his arms around her. Then one thing led to another until they were making love again. After it was over, she lay there completely happy and drifting off to sleep, thinking 'Whatever happens, this has been enough. More, much more.'

When she woke up, the sleeper was empty. She pulled on enough of her clothes to be decent and crawled into the cab, looking for the Duck. He was standing just outside the door with his hands on his hips staring up at the highway on the edge of the bluff. There, parked hood to tail along the shoulder of the road, was the longest line of trucks Melissa had ever seen. Even with the expanded field of view that the distance conferred, it stretched out of sight on both horizons. As in the original convoy, there were all kinds of vehicles involved, but the majority were big interstate diesels.

The Duck jumped back into the cab and reached for the CB. "Hey, anybody got a copy on me up there on that highway?" he called excitedly. "This here's the Rubber Duck. What're ya doin?'

"Waitin for you to finish your beauty sleep," came back a familiar voice. It was Pig Pen. Melissa felt suddenly as if she was going to cry. "Do you suppose you could get off your lazy ass long enough to come up here and take the front door of this thing? I been gettin just a heap of complaints from certain parties in my rockin chair here."

"You can just bet your sweet patootie on that," the Widow Woman came on. "First time I ever came close to bein assfixiated in my own truck."

"Widow Woman," Melissa broke in, "how did all this happen?"

"Oh, 'tweren't nothin really. After you all split this mornin, a bunch of us just started gabbing on the squawk box. And some of us had so much fun on the first convoy, we like to try it again. And some of the rest missed it first time around, so they was real disappointed. Once the Silver Streak and ole Baylor Benny found out where you was, it was easy. Come on up and let's get a move on. Them go-go girls is right near to doin me in."

"We'll be right there," Melissa cried. Then she realized what she'd said and turned to the Duck. "It's okay, isn't it?" she asked, ready to apologize for taking on too much. "I mean we are going, aren't we?"

He smiled and leaned over to give her a kiss. "It's better than that," he said, smiling that old insane smile she realized she hadn't seen for a long time. "We got us a *convoy*." He turned the ignition key and let her rip. And just from the way he fired up the engine, Melissa could see how very much it would take for him ever to stop again.

The junction of the secondary and the main highway was less than a mile away. As they drove slowly toward it, Melissa looked up at the line of vehicles awaiting them.

"This is just like approaching the 18th green at Augusta," she said.

"Seems more like approaching the head of a convoy in Texas," the Duck observed.

"Where will we be headed when we get there?" she asked, not wanting to pursue the argument.

The Duck shrugged. "The way we're headed as far as I can see. Maybe Washington wasn't such a bad idea."

"But what about the police?"

"Look, what we're gonna do is go. We'll let the Smokies figure out what to do with us, okay?"

They rode the rest of the way to the highway in silence. Melissa knew he hated being asked for answers he didn't have. But she retained an air of foreboding as they pulled upon the main road and took over the front door amid a chorus of air horns and excited chatter over the radio. As they accelerated to seventy and beyond, she found herself thinking, 'Now we really don't have anywhere else to go.'

CHAPTER TWELVE

MEANWHILE the convoy was now dealing with a new Governor in a new State. And at the state capital in Austin, Governor Clete Gryson was about to make that difference perfectly clear. A balding man in his fifties who had gone comfortably to paunch some years earlier, he was puffing on a cigar and talking on the phone at the same time in the approved Southern statehouse manner.

"Bet your sweet ass I'm calling out the Guard," he barked. "They aren't going to pull that shit in my state. And I want everything you can throw at em. Tanks, jeeps – and a goddamn jet. Get a goddamn phantom jet. Oh, and General, I want you to put Colonel Ridgeway in charge of the operation. I want this thing stopped fast, and I want it stopped right."

He hung up the phone and lit a fresh cigar although the other was only halfway smoked. He took a thoughtful puff or two to put himself in the proper frame of mind. Then he reached for the intercom button. "Okay, Miss Rogers. You can let those damned reporters in."

The National Guard Armory had become an anthill of activity as drivers ran to their trucks, rifles and flak jackets were issued, and noncoms zigzagged to and fro trying to issue orders. Suddenly, all the commotion died to an awed silence as two gigantic tanks rumbled through the assembly area toward the main gate.

"Jesus," one of the Guard men said as he gave his buddy a hand up into the personnel carrier, "this is gonna be some kind of operation."

"All I know is that I'm glad we're us and they're them," the buddy opined philosophically as the truck jolted into motion for the long trip west.

Out there, on a yet to be determined collision course, the convoy was tooling right along. Melissa turned on the AM radio, searching for a news report. She found one and turned the volume up to listen.

> "... At last report, the convoy was east of Norton City and still breaking all the speeding laws. Meanwhile there are reports that Governor Gryson has mobilized the National Guard. This has not been officially confirmed by the Governor's office as yet, but KYOL newsperson Jackson Wright reports seeing troops and equipment moving in the direction of Webber City. What their mission is, remains a mystery at this time. Elsewhere in the news ..."

Melissa switched off the radio and looked at the Duck, who continued staring impassively at the road ahead.

"Doesn't sound too promising," she observed.

"Yeah ..." the Duck agreed. He arrived at a sudden decision and reached for the mike.

"Break one-nine. Calling all trucks. This here is the Duck. I just heard on the radio that the Army got called out. I hate to say it, but you guys better think about scattering."

"Breaker. Breaker," a voice came on. "This is Pig Pen. What are *you* gonna do, Duck?"

"Drop my passenger off here, then try to make it to Mexico," the Duck said matter of factly, not looking at Melissa.

"Well, I'm sticking with you, Duck," Pig Pen came back. "It's been too good a haul. Besides, if worse comes to worse, we can always eat them go-go girls back there, providin anybody got the stomach for it."

"Breaker. This is Widow Woman sayin us, too. Bob here tells me it's real nice south of the border this time of year. Besides, we got to go somewhere on our honeymoon."

Melissa put her hand over the Duck's. "Me, too," she said in a soft, determined voice. "Your passenger is staying."

The Duck looked over at her with just the beginnings of a grin at the corners of his mouth. "I wouldn't recommend it," he warned.

Melissa shrugged, a mannerism of hers he was beginning

to find irresistible. "Neither would my mother," she answered stubbornly, "but I'm here for the duration."

"So what's the story, Duck?" Pig Pen cut in. "This here highway's gonna be hotter'n a June bride in a feather bed before much longer. You got any more of them back roads up your sleeve?"

The Duck was ready. For the past half-hour he and Melissa had been searching the Texas map for alternate routes.

"Take a right about a mile up here," he directed, "all of you that's goin. If I was you, I'd scatter though. There ain't enough bears in the whole state to handle you once you're split up."

He turned to Melissa. "One thing about any National Guard. They still gotta catch us."

She nodded her agreement, and crossed the fingers of her other hand.

Back in the mansion in Santa Fé, Governor Haskins was in the process of trying to get down the most bitter pill of his political career. As was often the case, Big Hank was with him to make sure he didn't shirk a grain. Big Hank was genuinely fond of the younger man. If he could be brought to learn from this experience while there was time to do something about it, he might still be saved. Big Hank poured himself another drink and waited. There were times when it didn't pay to push.

For the past five minutes, Haskins had sat silently behind his desk, staring political death squarely in the face. Finally, he brought himself back to the room to ask plaintively, "But *why* did they do it? I gave them everything they wanted."

"Because that's what those kind of people always do," Big Hank answered quickly. The time to strike had come. "No respect for authority. It's born in them. They take it in with their mother's milk."

"But wasn't I right?" the younger man countered in an almost pleading, uncertain voice.

"Right or wrong has nothing to do with it. They were breaking the law, and you are sworn to uphold the law. It's as simple as that."

"It can't be," the Governor protested. His voice was filled

with the horror of a dawning realization that probably it was.

Big Hank walked over until he was looking directly down into the shaken man's eyes. "It is," he declared.

Haskins broke the contact first. His head slumped down over the desk. He felt that he had always known that something like this was coming. He was a beaten man.

"What do you think we should do?" he asked in a tired, listless voice.

"Well, Gryson over in Texas is gonna stop em. You can bet on that. He's got the Guard out full force, and there's no way they can get by that." Big Hank's voice had become crisp, analytical. This was the kind of thing he handled well, and he knew it. "What we have to do right away is repudiate that agreement you made *before* the Guard picks them up. Because of a lack of good faith on their part, you are forced to rescind the order for amnesty and will take the other points under advisement at this time. That ought to do it for now."

"Isn't there any other way?" Haskins was going down for the third time and knew it.

"Not unless you want to find yourself lined up on the side of a bunch of convicted criminals. It's you or them."

After a moment of indecision, Haskins dialed Arnoldi's extension. "Hello, Chuck, this is Jerry Haskins," he said into the receiver, his voice becoming firmer, more determined with every word. "I've got an item for immediate release. I'm rescinding the amnesty. Yeah, that's right. Now, I'm counting on you to carry the ball on this one, Chuck. We've got to hit the wire services before they do."

The convoy had reached the southbound turnoff and started to divide. The majority of the vehicles proceeded straight ahead on their way to dispersing into the towns and secondaries to the east. A few of them pulled over to let the others get a lead on them. A nucleus of veterans plus one crazy kid driving a pickup out of El Paso followed the Duck off to the right.

Overhead and still unnoticed by the men below, a Texas State Police helicopter hovered, monitoring their every move. The pilot was on the radio to the lead car of a convoy of Army and police vehicles barely thirty miles to the east. The vehicle was occupied by agents Hamilton and Fish, Colonel Ridgeway, a career officer in the Guard, who looked as if he had been created from some subterranean mold at the Pentagon, and Lyle, who was heavily bandaged and sat staring morosely out the rear windwing. Somehow he had managed to retrieve his uniform, which was a little worse for the wear.

"They're coming up on the junction," the Pilot's voice sounded in the tense silence of the car. "The lead vehicle and a few of the others are turning now. Southbound on . . ."

"Is it a two-lane at the bottom of the valley there?" Hamilton asked. He was studying a map laid out across his knees.

"Yeah, that's it," the Pilot confirmed.

"Then it must be Decker Road," Hamilton came back. "Keep on em and stay out of sight if you can. Over and out."

Fish leaned over the back of the seat to get a better view. "They must be going south, like this," he said, tracing a route over the creased paper with his finger.

"Yes," Hamilton agreed, "And it looks like we could head them off here. You know this area, Colonel?"

"Sure. Folgersville," the Colonel replied in a somewhat incredible west Texas drawl. "You could block the bridge here. It's the best place for it."

"Then that's it," Hamilton decided. He began refolding the map.

Lyle bestirred himself to enter the conversation. "What about the jet?" he complained. "Ain't you goin to use the jet on em?"

Hamilton had had more than enough. He finished folding the map very deliberately and then turned in his seat to face Lyle full on.

"Wallace, let me remind you that you are here, over my most strenuous objections, solely for identification purposes. Your participation in either the planning or execution of this operation is not only not requested, but from his moment on, is expressly forbidden. Is that clear?"

"Yes *sir*," Lyle answered, his voice heavy with contempt.

"Furthermore, from what I hear about what you and your

bully pal did to that boy in Alvarez, I would personally enjoy nothing more than seeing that jet used on the both of you, for target practice."

Lyle humphed loud enough to blow a piece of snot onto the seat between him and Fish (who was reflecting that this was the last time he'd let Hamilton ride in the front) and settled back to contemplate his own anticipated vengeances.

"That was a little rough," Colonel Ridgeway said in low voice calculated to fall beneath the hum of the motor.

"Not half enough," Hamilton replied grimly. "The man's an asshole."

The Colonel took a look at Lyle in the rearview mirror and nodded his head at Hamilton sympathetically. Unfortunately, he had known the type.

What was left of the convoy continued rolling south under a gathering cloud of apprehension. By now the chopper had been spotted, but no one had yet been able to or willing to figure out what its presence meant.

"What do you want to do when this is all over?" Melissa asked to break the tension that was becoming more unbearable with every mile.

"You mean besides breaking rocks?" The Duck laughed at his own joke. "Back at the beginnin, I got into drivin sort of on a temporary basis. That was seventeen years ago and here I am."

She slid over and snuggled her head against his arm. "Here *we* are," she said.

The concrete span bridge that crossed the river outside of Folgersville was a little larger than appeared to be actually necessary, in order to handle the flashfloods that came pouring out of the nearby hills every spring and sometimes in the fall. Now it dwarfed the main channel, which was still carrying a fair amount of water for this time of summer. The generally undisturbed peace in which it soared over the river was disrupted by the arrival of a convoy of jeeps, personnel carriers, police vans, cruisers, and a riot control car complete with an M-60 machine gun mounted on its top. A distant sound of powerful engines further back down the road indicated that there was more to come.

There was no time to lose. Guardsmen spilled out of the covered trucks like streams of khaki water and, under the barking orders of their noncoms, began setting up barricades of concertina wire and positioning vehicles to block the road. The police contingent moved to the opposite side of the bridge and commenced setting itself up. Overhead an Army helicopter hovered in sputtering circles, monitoring the preparations and the surrounding terrain for possible loopholes of any kind.

All activity ceased suddenly as two mammoth tanks rolled into view and approached the bridge. There were M-60A2s, the most advanced prototypes, not usually assigned to the National Guard, but this was a crack unit, the best in Texas and sure to be the first called up in any national emergency.

The men simply stood where they were, staring, with tools or weapons dangling unnoticed from their hands while one of the tanks rumbled across the bridge and disappeared around a further curve. The other halted by the bridge abutment and started to position itself in the center of the road amid the chaos of vehicles and men.

"Come on, you leadasses," a noncom yelled when it was possible to be heard again. "We ain't got all day. Get those butts in gear. Whatsamatter, ain't you ever seen a tank before?"

While the tank crew completed its final course and range adjustment, the rest of the squad fanned out into the rocks and scrub on either side of the road.

"Damned if I know what we're doing here," one of them wondered aloud. "This ain't no war."

"Shut your face, man," his buddy ordered curtly. "Listen."

From the distance came the low-pitched rumble of powerful engines approaching rapidly like a summer storm.

The Duck was worried, mostly because nothing had happened. With that chopper up there, them bastards were holding all the cards. But as yet they hadn't played any, which meant, as far as he could see, that they were just biding their time. Which also meant, that he was driving straight for a trap, and there was nothing to do but keep his eyes and ears peeled and push right on into it.

"Breaker. Breaker," he called, "front door calling the back door. Got your ears on?"

"Yeah, I got you, Duck. Come on," Pig Pen answered. By unanimous vote he'd been moved to the rear after the main convoy split up because (1) he was one of the best back doors in the business, and (2) nobody could handle the backwash from those go-go girls after over a day on the road.

"Smell any smoke back there, Pig Pen?" the Duck asked.

"It's clean as far as I can see. What do you suppose they're doin?"

"Beats me. I'm gonna call out. Over." He paused for the conversation to clear and went back on the air. "Break one-nine. Calling any westbound eighteen-wheelers. Any of you westbound out there got a smokey report for the Rubber Duck and Company?"

"Ten-four, Rubber Duck," a distant voice came back. "This is the Iron Duke at marker . . ."

The words were suddenly blotted out by a piercing high-pitched whine. The Duck adjusted the squelch with no results. Then he flipped through all forty channels. The whining continued unaffected. He hit the radio with his hand a couple of times just in case something might be loose. Nothing changed. He flipped off the set and leaned back with a worried look on his face.

"What happened?" Melissa asked, her voice husky with fear.

"They're jammin our signals. I can't get through to anybody."

They entered a wooded, hilly area of winding, twisting curves, sharp enough that each of the trucks lost contact with the others while negotiating them. The convoy began to string out with close to twenty yards between vehicles. With their CBs jammed, the drivers began feeling more and more alone. Something was going to happen. But what?

"Duck . . ." Melissa said suddenly.

"Uh-huh."

"I'm worried."

He gave her a tense smile. "Don't feel like the Lone Ranger."

She watched him drive for a moment and then said quietly. "But I don't regret a minute of it, Duck. Not a minute."

He bent across the seat and answered her with a kiss. In his eyes, she could see what she knew was shining out of her own. It was settled. He loved her.

On the top of a bluff around the next curve a Guard Captain spotted them coming. It was perfect. There was at least fifteen yards between the lead truck and the second in line. He raised his arm to signal the tank concealed on the side road below. As the Duck's truck passed the intersection, the tank roared out onto the highway and began pursuing it down the road, strewing large chunks of asphalt like pebbles from its giant treads. There was nothing that the Widow Woman, who was driving second, could do but follow helplessly behind. The Duck was cut off, isolated between the tank and whatever lay ahead.

The Duck downshifted for power and put the pedal down, easily outdistancing the tank. In no time, he was a couple of hundred yards head and pulling away. He was getting all that the rig had to give, his tires squealing as they rounded every curve. Too terrified to scream, Melissa clutched the door handle and hung on. They pulled around the final curve before the bridge. With a curse of surprise the Duck stood on the brakes and skidded to a stop with the trailer three-quarters of the way to jackknifing behind him.

Before the dust had completely settled, the pursuing tank roared to a stop behind the truck and sat there idling, apparently content simply to cut off any escape to the rear. Behind the tank, the rest of the convoy was stacked up helplessly out of the action. All they could do now was watch – and pray. In the abrupt silence that settled over the scene, the giant machines seemed to be holding each other at bay like prehistoric animals.

The police P.A. suddenly sounded from across the river: "Surrender. Surrender immediately or you will be fired on."

Inside the cab, the Duck turned to Melissa. Now more

than ever, her thoroughbred good looks seemed woefully out of place. It had been a fool's dream, their being together beyond the few moments they had already shared, he suddenly realized. She should be photographing this action, not part of it.

"You better get out," he said softly.

The only evidence of the shock she had to be feeling was the slightest narrowing of her eyes.

"What are you going to do?" she asked, needing but not really wanting to know. There was no good answer to her question, and she knew it.

As she waited for him to speak, Melissa noticed how tired the Duck had become, not just from the events of the last couple of days, but from the years and miles on the road, too many miles, strange women, strong drink they had creased his face like a map. She had the sudden, irrational feeling that if only she had the time, she could follow each wrinkle and line to its ultimate source at the marrow of his life.

The Duck's amphetamine – triggered eyes darted back and forth over the situation like a snake's tongue, but he only said: "Better go."

"You will be fired upon unless you surrender," the P.A. broke in. "You have ten seconds. One . . . two . . ."

The Duck cracked the door on Melissa's side of the cab and pushed her gently toward it

"But what are you going to do, Duck?" she demanded half hysterically as part of the answer he began to hit her.

He took in the scene one more time – the tanks, the police, the squad of men lining the road. Then his eyes came back to hers, asking her to understand.

"Keep on truckin. Now git."

"Seven . . . eight . . ."

Slowly, feeling very old and useless, Melissa climbed out of the cab and walked away. She heard the door slam behind her but didn't look back. She didn't want to see what was coming.

Pig Pen and the Widow Woman came running up to her, followed at various distances by Big Nasty and the rest of the truckers.

"What's he doin?" Pig Pen panted. "What's goin on?"

Melissa spread her hands helplessly.

"My God," the Widow Woman breathed. She put her arms around Melissa to steady her.

"Goddamn, goddamn, goddamn," Pig Pen kept intoning to himself in an agonized monotone. He wanted to do something, to scream – what?

"Ten," the voice on the P.A., which had slowed down its final count, rasped. "This is your last chance. Come out with your hands over your head."

The tense silence was broken by a sudden Indian warhoop that jerked Melissa around to face the scene like a gigantic, compelling hand. Whatever she might have said or even thought was drowned out by the roar of four hundred diesel horses as the Duck put the hammer down. She watched in frozen fascination as the black Mack shot forward charging certain death – the tank directly ahead.

Inside the tank, Corporal Elton Beauregard racked his .50 caliber M-1 HMG and prepared to fire. The crazy son of a bitch was going to get blown away, right now. The radio crackled, "This is Colonel Ridgeway. Hold your fire. This is a police action. I repeat, do not fire unless ordered to do so."

Corporal Beauregard eased his pressure on the trigger. "Shit," he complained regretfully.

As the truck approached the bridge, the Duck threw himself to the floor of the cab, steering blindly with one hand. If he had calculated correctly, there might be just enough room.

Almost miraculously, the truck wedged cleanly between the tank and the retaining wall of the bridge, striking both at once and tearing off its fenders and doors. But somehow it was through and heading across the bridge toward the scattering police forces on the far side.

Almost immediately, the M-60 machine gun mounted on the riot car opened up. In a matter of seconds the Mack's windshield appeared and steam began pouring from its punctured radiator. But it kept coming with no sign of slowing despite the terrible punishment it was moving through.

Inside the cab, a bullet had ripped through the Duck's arm, but intent on steering and punching the gas pedal, he felt no pain or fear. A pure perfect rage was his shield against all that.

There was a sudden commotion at the base of the riot car as Lyle, who was halfway up the side, tried to jerk himself free from the tenacious grip that Hamilton had fastened on one of his boots and take over the gun. With a last spurt of panic-stricken energy Lyle smashed the heel of his free foot into the other man's temple and broke loose.

He elbowed the Highway Patrolman off to the side and centered the sights of the M-60 on the *VOLATILE CHEMICALS* sign stenciled across the leading edge of the Duck's trailer. "Blow, you asshole," he grunted as he pressed the firing mechanism, etching a line of holes through the center of the sign.

The resulting explosion was only slightly less than nuclear.

A fireball sprinkled with pieces of truck, bridge, wheels, mushroomed a good forty feet into the air above the river. The clearing smoke revealed nothing but the burning remains of the trailer. The cab, which had broken loose just before the explosion, had been thrown through the metal guard rail and now rested somewhere beneath the rocking surface of the river. The Convoy was over.

Police, Guardsmen and truckers rushed as one body to the gaping hole in the rail. The dark water revealed nothing. The cab had disappeared completely from sight. Melissa began crying hysterically. Pig Pen and the Widow Woman held her between them for comfort, but their eyes, too, were wet with shock and loss.

A jeep carrying Colonel Ridgeway came roaring up and screeched to a halt. "Get some men in that water," he ordered. "Get hold of some grappling hooks."

Hamilton watched with the rest as the makeshift divers went down and resurfaced again and again with no results.

"My God," he murmured to Fish, who was standing shakily beside him, "what have we done?"

EPILOGUE

On the whole, Governor Haskins was having, if not exactly a good, then a satisfying time. Generally, he didn't like funerals, but this one had more the character of a State occasion. And there was also the fact that he was a hero to those thousands of voters lining the streets on either side of the procession. Naturally, he had been given the position of honor, the limousine directly behind the one carrying the immediate family. He glanced ahead at the rubber duck, which seemed to be bouncing almost gaily on the top of the casket. Was he mocking it, or it mocking him?

He punched Big Hank in the ribs with his elbow and said, "Don't look so disapproving, Henry. Those are your constituents out there, you know."

But despite his political calling, Big Hank was more a man of principle than that. He maintained a sturdy disgust for the whole damn proceeding and the expression in his face altered not a bit.

Oh well. The Governor sat back to savor once more the complex of ironies that had brought him to where he was today and very likely back to the Governor's mansion for another term once November rolled around. And after that, who knew? He was a political hero now, both in and out of the state, if the deluge of speaking invitations already pouring in was to be believed. And he owed it all to Arnoldi. That had to be one of the ultimate ironies of the century, if not for all time.

When the news of his death had been flashed across the country by the media, the Rubber Duck had become not only an instant hero, but even more so, a cause. National reaction had divided almost evenly between the guilt of those who were in authority and the anger of those who weren't.

Full-scale riots sprang up in several major cities as the

people took out their frustration and grief on the society that had condemned the man they had taken as their leader to death. Bumper stickers proclaiming DAMN THE DOUBLE NICKEL appeared almost instantaneously, and throughout the country, vehicles of all descriptions began banding together in convoys traveling well over the posted fifty-five. A state patrolman pulled over a trucker in a little Arkansas town and was promptly set upon and thrashed by a crowd of angry bystanders. Within two days, Woolworth's was completely sold out of rubber ducks and dispatched a rush cable to Hong Kong for fifty-thousand more.

The establishment response had been equally swift and to the point. A day of mourning was proclaimed by fully two-thirds of the state legislatures. Patrolmen were instructed to travel in pairs and to forget about their monthly citation quotas for the time being. Several state referendums patterned on what had come to be known as the 'New Mexico Model' had been established nationwide, and there was talk in Washington of taking a hard look at the fifty-five mile per hour limit – and the profit structure of the major oil companies – when Congress reconvened in the fall. The price of gasoline had actually dropped a couple of cents in many areas with vague promises from the major producers of further reductions in the future.

And except for Arnoldi's basic incompetence, he might have ended upon the wrong side of all this, the Governor reflected with a shudder. For by the time Arnoldi had gotten together the release and notified the reporters of the impending press conference, the news of the Duck's death was on every radio, TV set and voter's tongue. It had been a simple matter for the Governor to tear up his prepared statement in favor of an eloquent impromptu reaffirmation of his original pact with the convoy. His speech, which brought a tear to more than one eye, had been carried by all the major networks and quoted widely in the press.

'Good old Chuck,' the Governor reflected as his glance fell on the vacant passenger seat that ordinarily Arnoldi would have occupied on an occasion such as this. Fools had their uses, but it was too dangerous to count on their ineptitude rebounding to your credit every time.

As the limousine slowed for an intersection, an old lady leaning on a cane hobbled out to it. "God bless you, Governor," she cried through the partly open window. "You was the only one to give those boys a fair shake."

Taking care to keep his smile within acceptable limits, the Governor reached through the window to shake her withered hand.

"It's a sad day," he intoned mournfully. "A sad day for us all."

He sat back wishing that this damn procession would break up pretty soon. He needed a nice, strong drink.

Hamilton wandered restlessly through the crowd, looking for he didn't know what. He had requested and been granted special leave to attend the funeral, but now that he was here, he couldn't begin to understand why he had felt compelled to come.

After hours of dragging the river had failed to turn up the Duck's body, he had caught a plane back to Gallup, courtesy of the National Guard. His wife had been asleep when he arrived home, but after he had finished his third consecutive cigarette sitting up in bed and running the events of the past two days through his mind like a mad projectionist, she waked up and rolled over to look at him.

"I saw it on the TV," he said. "Was it very bad?"

He nodded. "Elaine, I'm going to ask for leave to go to the funeral wherever it is."

She had studied him for a long time, noted the determination that was driving him.

"I think you should," she had decided. "Now, put out the light and try to get some sleep."

But sleep hadn't come that night, nor had it been easy in the days that followed. Like most FBI men, Hamilton was motivated by a strong sense of justice and duty. In this case, although he had received an official commendation from the office, he was strangely unable either to justify his actions or to see what else he might have done. Maybe that was why he was here – to find some reasons that would give him peace.

He felt a hand on his shoulder and turned to confront a familiar face.

"Fish," he cried excitedly, "what are you doing here?"

The other man gave him a wan smile. "The same thing you are," he answered. "What is it?"

Hamilton shook his head slowly. "I don't know. I just keep seeing those pieces of truck floating through the air and hearing that poor girl scream."

Fish nodded. "Well, we could always try to find Lyle and beat the hell out of him. It probably wouldn't do any good, but it sure would be satisfying."

Hamilton chuckled wryly at the thought. "And there's not even any way to put that son of a bitch behind bars," he marveled. "Makes you wonder what side you're really on."

Fish reached into his pocket, pulled out a nickel and poised it on his thumb. "Call it in the air," he said. "Loser buys coffee in that diner across the street."

Hamilton called heads and lost. As he followed Fish's lead through the thinning crowd, he told himself that even if there weren't any real answer here that he could see, maybe the questions would begin to seem a little less overwhelming in the years to come.

Intent on their own thoughts, the two men passed within a yard of Melissa and old Mrs. Jackson without noticing. Melissa had finished her story and was crying, the large soft tears streaming down her face while the old lady stood helplessly by.

"What a tragedy, what a terrible tragedy," she said, trying to make some kind of effort at consolation. "He must have been someone very special."

"Yes, he was," Melissa managed to choke out. "I loved him." She indicated the crowd around them with a sweep of her arm. "They all loved him. He was the greatest trucker that ever lived."

"Yeah, and he ain't too bad at swimmin' either," came a voice from the crowd beyond them.

From the stunned, incredulous, joyful look on Melissa's face, the old lady knew who it was, had to be. She had just time for a glimpse of a tall, well built man with one arm in a sling and wearing a huge sombrero that covered his face, before Melissa spun, cameras flying, to throw herself into one of the happiest hugs the old woman had ever seen. Melissa was crying even harder than before, but there was laughter too, and the kind of incoherent babbling that only two lovers really understand.

Across the street, a figure masquerading as a tourist stiffened to attention. Hot damn, this was it. Lyle had been following Melissa around Albuquerque for three days just waiting for something like this. He'd had his suspicions all along, and it looked like he'd finally hit the jackpot. Course he couldn't be sure with that big hat the fella was wearing, but from the way she was hugging up to him, there wasn't just a shitload of doubt in his mind.

Not that there was anything he could do about it right here and now anyway. If this crowd got a whiff of who he was, Lyle knew they'd tear him apart just for the fun of it. But he'd find out, if not today, tomorrow, or the next day. He had the patience to wait – and the hate to make it all worthwhile.

After the two young people had disappeared joyfully into the crowd, old Mrs. Jackson started home, her step more sprightly than it had been for years. She smiled to herself. Perhaps there was something truly mysterious and magical to this thing called life. She felt as though she'd known it all along.

She passed by a TV newsman, who she could not have known was Dave Raymond making his final report before heading for his new assignment at the main network offices in New York.

"... but as we mourn the passing of the Rubber Duck, there is a happy irony to be found in the story," he was saying seriously into the mini cam. "The truckers were here today by the hundreds to honor their fallen leader in a procession the like of which this country has seldom, if ever, seen." He looked up and down the emptying street as if expecting something. Almost in answer to his glance, there was a distant rumble of engines as the last of the procession made its way out of town. "The Duck is gone," he concluded thoughtfully, "but here at his funeral, the convoy lives on."

THE END